Acclaim for *Local Music*

In *Local Music*, Cummins writes about love in all its dangerous permutations, its complements and contraries, its triangles and traps, bright sides and undersides—and he does so in a prose so clean that the page disappears and the stories play like movies in the mind. His characters are rendered with such authenticity, so nuanced, that you'd swear they're related to you; he captures the subtle turns that render attachment, and its attendant, nearly macabre unkindnesses, visible and unforgettable. The music in *Local Music*? In Cummins, love is the local music, its rapture and calamity, abrasion and improvisation, the brilliant local music of what makes love love.

> —Renée Ashley, prize-winning author of *The Revisionist's Dream*, *The Various Reasons of Light, Salt, and Someplace Like This*

The stories in *Local Music* are spare, beautifully written, and always haunting—in the best sense. Walter Cummins's characters are ambushed by the circumstances of their lives. They struggle with anger, loneliness, and disappointment, and sometimes stumble into joy. This is a startling and expertly crafted collection. The stories stayed with me long after I finished this powerful book.

> —Ronna Wineberg, author of *Second Language*, winner of the Many Voices Project

Local Music is a stunning panorama of the human species, with its many oddities, aspirations, frustrations, anguishes, and hopes.

> —Jack Smith, Co-editor, *The Green Hills Literary Lantern*

The stories in Local Music limn the secret self's perverse longings and superstitions, as they uncover the alienation wrought by those mysteries. Cummins' insight into his characters is revelatory, his prose sharp and devastating. These are memorable, moving stories, full of satisfying surprises and beautiful strangeness.

> —René Steinke, author of *The Fires* and *Holy Skirts,* a 2005 National Book Awards finalist

In *Local Music*, his third collection of short fiction, Walter Cummins once again conjures up luminous prose to plot what drives his lively cast of anti-heroes and anti-heroines through life. In story after story his characters are on the move, sometimes physically and sometimes metaphorically, trying to escape from each other and even from themselves; their world may seem poised to come crashing down about them, yet they soldier doggedly on. Don't look for happy Hollywood endings here; traveling as they do through a bleak landscape, and coping as they go, Walter Cummins' protagonists have to create their own sunshine. Seventeen stories to ponder, one at a time.

> —Victor Rangel-Ribeiro, author of *Loving Ayesha* and *Tivolem*, winner of the Milkweed Prize for Fiction

Books by Walter Cummins

Story Collections
Habitat: stories of bent realism
The Lost Ones
The End of the Circle
Local Music
Where We Live
Witness

Novels
A Stranger to the Deed
Into Temptation

Nonfiction
The Literary Traveler, with Thomas E. Kennedy
Programming Our Lives: Television and American Identity,
with George Gordon
Managing Management Climate, with George Gordon
Florham: The Lives of an American Estate,
with Carol Bere and Samuel Convissor

Edited
The Book of Worst Meals, with Thomas E. Kennedy
Writers on the Job, with Thomas E. Kennedy
Shifting Borders: East European Poetry of the Eighties
The Other Side of Reality: Myths, Vision & Fantasies,
with Martin Green and Margaret Verhulst

www.waltercummins.com

Local Music

STORIES

WALTER CUMMINS

A Nine Lives
Edition

SERVING HOUSE BOOKS

Local Music

ISBN: 978-0-9858495-9-7

Cover image: Created by Walter Cummins with images from 123rf.com

Serving House Books logo by Barry Lereng Wilmont

A Nine Lives Edition
Published by Serving House Books
Copenhagen, Denmark and Florham Park, NJ

www.servinghousebooks.com

Originally published by Egress Books 2007

First Serving House Books Edition 2014

To Tom Kennedy for friendship and collaboration

Thanks to the Two Bridges Writers' Group for years of good advice and to Alison for taming my verbal excesses

Additional thanks to Marty Flowers for wise and perceptive editorial proofreading

Acknowledgments

Original versions of these stories first appeared in the following publications:

"Local Music" and "Riding West," *Georgetown Review*

"Escaping this Place" and "Gone," *North Atlantic Review*

"Homemaking," "Handyman," and "Brother," *Green Hills Literary Lantern*

"Visiting," *Crosscurrents*

"Pleasure," *Del Sol Review*

"Clogged," *Florida Review*

"Petrushka," *Crescent Review*

"Trap," *This: a Serial Review*

"Fathering," *Dominion Review*

"Ten Years" and "Hiding Place," *Connecticut Review*

"Islands," *Sonora Review*

"Little Old Man," *Bellevue Literary Review*

Contents

Local Music

The sax player bent back at the knees and made an abrupt switch from hard bop to free jazz, bleating guttural low notes, emitting high, painful screeches, a dark little man with a battered face, so small the tenor in his hands seemed like a baritone. A fierce looking young woman, half his age and four inches taller, wearing all black, straddled a chair beside him and jerked her head to the dissonance. She had appeared his second week in town, fetching him beers from the bar, holding his cigarette when he soloed, sucking long drags and scowling at the audience.

Philip sat alone at the table he took every night, watching the bewilderment of the drummer and bass player, local musicians whose only experience had been weddings and high school dances. Now they were accompanying a pro, Bobo Grissom, a man once famous in New York, until heroin made him too unreliable for regular work. It felt odd to Philip to be sitting in this bar, the Rusty Spike, that for years had nothing but a Nashville-sound juke box, and hear live improvisations from a man whose old records were collector's items. Amid the familiar sawdust floor, patched-felt pool table, and flashing beer signs, the notes jarred, signals that he had drifted into some strange place.

Philip locked his gaze on the musicians, unwilling to face the empty chair across the table, the spot where Annie had always sat, smiling back at him, loose strands of hair glittering in the light, her face so animated it seemed the heart of the evening. If he didn't look, maybe she would suddenly materialize, reach out to touch his hand.

To stop the thought he wondered how much they were paying Bobo, beyond the use of a room upstairs and a diet of hamburgers and pulpy fries. That was the kind of puzzle he allowed to absorb him: counting the customers in the bar, the price of a beer, multiplying to estimate an average night's take, subtracting salaries and overhead. There couldn't be much left. Of all the choices in the world, why had Bobo Grissom ended up here, soloing for hours each night in front of an audience that couldn't tell Doc Severensen from Miles Davis and earning pennies for his efforts?

Philip saw Billy Pealskin wandering about the bar with a bottle and a glass as if searching for a table, even though the room was half empty. Before Philip could look away, Billy caught his eye and sat down next to him.

"Why does he do it, Billy?" Philip pointed toward Bobo.

"Do what?" Billy was a clean-featured young man, muscular from weight lifting, dressed in a fresh shirt and work pants, always wearing a knitted cap pulled down to his ears to hide a patchy white baldness, great clumps of hair missing because of some untreatable scalp disease. People avoided him, women especially, perhaps, Philip thought, less because of his hair than his remote eyes, the feeling that he was obsessed with a subject you couldn't imagine.

"Play his heart out in front of hicks."

"Maybe he likes listening to himself."

"Then he's luckier than most of us," Philip said.

Billy cocked his head, as if he were focused on the music. But Philip knew he wasn't. "How come you're not pissed," Billy finally said.

"About what?"

"Annie and Stan?"

"What good would being pissed do?"

"She's your wife, man. He's supposed to be your friend."

Once Philip had suspected Billy was infatuated with Annie, always hovering near their table in the Spike, cutting across the street just to say hello. Then he realized it was only envy, that Billy was drawn to any woman who seemed to love a man. "That happens a lot, doesn't it?" he said. "Wives and best friends."

"Don't you hate the fucker?"

"What good's hating?"

"He's screwing her, man!" Billy slammed his bottle on the table top, and Bobo's girl shot him a look, though the sax player's eyes were closed as he let out a series of staccato honks.

Philip couldn't picture Annie and Stan in bed. Whenever he thought about them, he imagined them walking the streets of the town in an unending analysis of their relationship — if they truly had one, what they would do next if they did. He had seen them together once, a block away, both in heavy coats, hands in pockets, not touching though they moved side by side, Stan a hulking man with a pigeon-toed walk, Annie in fur-lined boots stepping quickly to keep up with his pace. Once the three of them used to spend hours together in his living room, the cassette deck playing in a perpetual loop, Annie and Philip holding hands on the couch, Stan stretched on the floor, his back propped against a chair, occasionally bringing a date that Philip ended up amusing while Stan and Annie got into an intense argument. They disputed everything — politics, movies, food — so much that Philip suspected they despised each other, until the night in this bar, the Rusty Spike, Stan, drunk, tears glistening on his cheeks, confessed that he loved her. "And does Annie love you?" Philip had asked, calm, as if talking about strangers. "We're working that one out," Stan had said.

Actually, there may not have been any sex yet; but Philip didn't want to say that to Billy. He had decided that it was best not to know, even though he sensed that Annie was eager for him to ask. Which satisfaction did she want: bragging of her ecstasies or her abstentions? Perhaps his satisfaction was not asking, avoiding the subject each time she called him to meet for coffee, talking through so many refilled cups that afterwards he lay awake all night with electric nerves. For all their thousands of words, he had no idea what they were discussing: emotions, loyalties, needs. What did any of it mean?

In the apartment, she had the bedroom, and he slept on the couch, neither of them home till late at night, eating out separately, meeting on the way to the bathroom with muttered "Excuse me's." All their conversations took place on neutral territory — diners and parking lots, their exchanges very civilized, neither raising a voice. Her revelations sounded as patterned as music, with him groping to keep up, like the other local players. Sometimes Philip wondered how it would feel to emulate Bobo and just scream bursts of noise.

Philip felt the table shaking and looked up just as Billy seized his wrist and started tugging at him, mouth contorted, suddenly furious. "You sonofabitch! You dumb sonofabitch!"

Philip flinched back, expecting to be hit. "What's wrong, Billy? What's going on?"

"Annie's a great woman, and you don't even give a shit."

"Sure I care. But what do you expect me to do? You can't force a person to love you."

"Kick Stan's ass! Drag the bastard through the fucking gutter."

"What if that made her hate me?"

"She'd respect you, you asshole!"

"Maybe somebody like her would." Philip gestured toward Bobo's girlfriend. "But you don't know Annie."

"That one's a slut. If I lost a woman like Annie, I'd kill myself."

Bobo was sitting next to the girl now, wiping the sweat from his face with a bandanna, shoving an end of the cloth down under his shirt. She held a cigarette to his lips for him to inhale. The drummer was taking a toneless solo, thumping, clanging cymbals, beating sticks against a metal edge.

Billy dropped Philip's arm and clamped his hands to his ears, then rose to his feet and shouted, "Cut that noise!"

For an instant the drummer paused, sticks high over his head. Philip expected him to hurl them and ducked. But the man just pounded more loudly.

When Philip looked, Bobo's girl was heading for their table, the heels of her studded black boots clicking on the wooden floor. She stood in front of Billy, her scowl inches from his face, then pressed down on both his shoulders and forced him back into his chair. Bobo was studying his spit valve.

"Shut your mouth, fuzz head," she hissed at Billy.

Billy slowly took one of her hands from his shoulder and lay it across his left palm, measuring how much shorter and thinner her fingers were, stroking her long red nails. She watched in puzzlement, shared a glance with Philip. Then Billy began to squeeze, his jaw clenched, neck flushed, tendons taut.

He'll crush the bones, Philip thought and began pulling at Billy's arm, tried to pry open his fingers. "Billy, stop."

The girl screamed.

Philip heard a vibration, the bass set on the floor, and saw the bass player rushing toward them, the drummer beating wildly, Bobo sprawled back in his chair, the bandanna spread over his face. The bass player was a big, flabby man, long haired, large nosed, a growth of stubble on jowls that sagged into his shirt collar. He drove a fist into Billy's back, hit him again and again until Billy dropped the girl's hand.

She winced, shook her wrist, sucked her fingertips. "Fuzzhead bastard!"

When Billy lunged toward her, the bass player blocked him with a forearm. Billy reached for the chair, but the man knocked it away.

"What's your name?" Billy asked him, suddenly calm, readjusting his knitted cap.

The bass played glared at him. "Chet," he finally said. "How long have you lived in this town? Don't you know anything?"

"I know I'm Billy. And I forget you already, asshole." Billy snapped his jacket and walked to the front door, kicked it open, and disappeared out onto the street.

"Crazy bastard." Chet stared at Philip as if Billy were his fault.

Philip shrugged and the man walked away.

Now the girl stood behind Bobo, draping her arms over his chest, holding her hand up to his mouth. She rubbed his lips just as the drummer, hair snaking over his forehead, ended his solo by coming down on foot pedal, snare, and cymbals in one final slam. A few people applauded, Philip among them, and the musicians disappeared behind the bar, the girl still holding onto Bobo, pressing against his back as they moved, her chin on his head.

Philip was jarred by the abrupt silence until the bartender snapped on the TV suspended over a shelf of liquor bottles and somebody dropped coins into the juke box. He watched basketball players run up and down the court, the announcers drowned out by twanging guitars.

13

Just for something to do, he got up to buy himself another beer.

As he turned to walk back to his table, Annie and Stan came through the front door. Philip froze waiting for one of them to notice him; but they took a table close to the window without looking in his direction.

Stan stood behind Annie to slip her coat off, draped it over the back of her chair. It was her alpaca jacket, the one she had coveted for months before deciding to buy, then hung in the closet in a garment bag because it was too good for ordinary wear. Now, though Stan tried to be careful, the sleeves dragged on the floor. He unzipped his jacket but did not take it off. Before he sat, he signaled one of the bartenders and had two beers served on a tray.

Finally, after several minutes of anxious waiting, Philip went back to his chair. They knew he would be at the Spike, avoiding the apartment until it was too late to stay awake any longer. And this was the first time they had come there since Stan's confession. They must have wanted to see him. Perhaps they had made a decision. Something was going to happen. Philip wrapped a hand around the beer bottle, then touched his chilled fingers to his forehead. His legs were trembling under the table.

Still they did not seem to see him, did not even search the room for a glimpse of him. They were leaning forward, not speaking, just looking at each other.

Philip tried to read their eyes from a distance, but he couldn't tell if they were locked in a gaze of love or one of regret. Had they decided they had no future, that she should go back to her life with him? Was this their way of saying farewell? Would they finish the drink and have Stan slip away, out to the street, leaving her alone, certain that he, Philip, would move forward to sit beside her? Or were they working up the nerve to tell him he had lost his wife?

The musicians returned, Bobo now playing in his old style from years ago, the rhythm driving and the melody clear, standard tunes, Cole Porter, the Gershwins, embellished with improvisations, but rooted in familiar patterns.

Although he knew the impossibility even as he thought it, Philip imagined Annie and Stan had requested these songs, that their playing was a message to him, one he failed to decipher. A nostalgic requiem or a return to order?

It was crazy, all this speculation. They were thirty feet away. He only had to get up and ask them what was happening to their lives, yet he couldn't make himself move. He pressed down on the edge of the table to pull himself up, but instead tilted it toward him and knocked the bottle on its side, foam spreading across the gouged wood. People turned to look, but not Annie and Stan.

I will get up, I will get up, he kept saying to himself. Forcing himself to his feet, he took one step toward them and veered away toward the musicians, finding himself in front of Bobo's girl, thinking that she was hard and ugly, that when he was Bobo's age he wouldn't want to end up with somebody like her.

"Well?" she said, slapping the back of the chair she straddled, ready to dismiss him with a sneer.

"I have some of his old LPs," Philip thought to say, wondering if Annie and Stan were staring at his back now. "Music just like this."

"So?"

"Do you think he'd autograph them if I brought them in sometimes."

"He might charge you."

"What?"

"Bobo's in demand these days."

Philip nodded. "Ok. I'll pay if I have to."

"Get away from me," she hissed. "Away!"

When Philip turned, he saw that Billy was back, sitting close to Annie, huddled on a chair he had dragged up beside her. He had his back to Stan, smiling at her, a hand posed in mid-air, as if he were about to stroke her face. Philip had the sensation that the hand was his own, that he had only to reach out and make everything right.

When Chet went into a bass solo, slapping and plucking, Billy wheeled around in the chair, rose to his feet. He cupped a hand to his mouth and shouted. "Shut the fuck up!" Annie touched his arm to calm him. Billy seized her hand and held it to his lips. Philip looked

15

to Stan for a reaction. He seemed annoyed, but Annie did not pull her hand away.

Then Billy dropped it and walked back directly to Philip, even though Philip was shaking his head. You'll spoil everything, he mouthed. But Billy took a chair and slid it close, as close as he had been to Annie.

He hunched over the table and parted his coat, nudging Philip to look inside. laughing and nodding rapidly. "See! See!"

It took Philip several seconds to adjust his vision and realize that it was a pistol butt showing over the edge of an inside pocket, shiny and silver. "Jesus, Billy! Where'd that come from?"

Billy wrapped his fingers around the metal and laughed again. "Don't think I don't know how to shoot the sucker."

"I bet you can, Billy. You're probably an expert." He was sure Annie and Stan were watching him now, and he didn't know what he should do.

Billy drew out the pistol, so small in his large fingers that only the glitter showed. Then he held it out at arm's length, pointing toward the front of the bar.

He's going to kill Stan, Philip thought. He swallowed and tried make himself shout a warning. But the sound locked in his throat. He reached out with trembling hands.

But Billy was already on his feet, rushing forward, though not at Stan. He swerved toward Chet, letting out a howl that overwhelmed the music. Chet, head down, kept picking at the bass as if he had not heard. Bobo, eyes squeezed, thrust out his horn and screamed a melody. But the drummer dropped his sticks and the girl hoisted her chair as if it were a shield.

Philip watched Billy aim, taking his time, sighting down the stubby barrel. No! No! No! The unspoken shout echoed through his mind, dissonant, out of tune, as if he were another player who didn't belong. He cringed and waited for the explosion.

From behind, Stan wrapped Billy in a bear hug, pinning his arms, knocking off his knit cap to expose the strange splotched head. The pistol spun loose and skittered across the floor boards until Bobo's girl stepped on it with a black boot.

Philip turned away and met Annie's eyes. When he saw the tears, he let himself cry with her.

Riding West

When Peter turned the corner and found Denise waiting at the curb with three suitcases, he leaned out the window, not sure whether to be amused or annoyed. "Hey! It's only two weeks." His own few changes of clothes were rolled up inside an old duffle bag thrown in the trunk.

"You never can tell," she said.

"What you're going to need?"

"Where you'll end up."

He couldn't figure out why she was wearing stockings, high heels, a red sleeveless dress, carrying a small white purse. They could have been going across town to a party, not setting off for four long days on the interstate, heading west in an old Escort with a deep gouge rusting down the passenger's door. He glanced in the rearview mirror and caught an edge of his unshaven jaw, then glanced down at his tee shirt, jeans, and flapping sandals. What a mismatched pair they'd make sitting side by side for hundreds of miles.

Peter got out to load two of her suitcases into the trunk. The biggest had to slide onto the back seat; he strained to lift it but didn't ask what she had inside. Then she sat in the car and waited for him to shut her door.

•

If he'd kept his mouth shut, this wouldn't be happening, Peter thought — traveling across the country with a stranger to a place he wasn't sure he wanted to see again. But one night after work when everybody was pouring from pitchers of beer and talking about vacations, someone asked Peter about his plans. Usually he just sat back and listened to the others. Answering was his mistake, nervously blurting intentions for a trip he had planned in detail but never expected to take: drive west for several days to a town on the Coast he had lived in once, visit familiar places, perhaps look up a few people. That was what he told them, though he was sure it would never happen despite the hours he had wasted in daydreaming.

As Peter was speaking, Denise arrived from her job a few blocks away, taking the empty chair across the table from him next to Glenn, her husband. "I've been thinking of a trip west myself. I'll ride with you," she said, not asking, just stating a fact. "Split the gas and the driving. It'll save us time and money." "What about you?" Peter looked at Glenn, hoping he would be going too, but Glenn shrugged. "Not a good time for me." Peter felt his scalp prickling. "It's an old car that's been having problems," he told Denise. "The cylinder head, I think." She had smiled, bright lip gloss flecked on her teeth. "I'll take my chances."

•

So here they were. Peter concentrated on the driving, maneuvering through the thick traffic in the center of town, taking a shortcut through the industrial park, and coming out to the highway. He started to apologize for the condition of the Escort — the back floor littered with plastic grocery bags, crushed cans, tattered sneakers — then changed his mind. Denise didn't say a word, looking out at the local scenery as if she were a tourist. This was the first time Peter had ever been alone with her.

He and Glenn did data entry in the same office. The work called for concentration and left little time for small talk. Some days they ate lunch together or went for a beer; Denise joined them now and then, part of a group chattering over sports or the weather or government stupidities. He knew nothing about their lives.

Glenn was OK, Peter thought all along, but he'd never had a reaction to Denise until they were sitting next to each other one evening at a big round table and she pressed her leg against his, tight from calf to thigh. He reached across for a pitcher of beer to break the contact, but she shifted with him. Peter wouldn't meet her eyes, didn't know what to do next. He suspected that if he dropped his hand to her knee, she would seize it, rub it up and down. Then what? He realized that he didn't want to know.

Her look didn't appeal to him — round olive face, flat features, thick lips, dark lidded eyes, heavy calves. But she carried herself like a femme fatale, and he could see men responding, as if to an invitation of a secret smoldering, a promise of unimagined delights. For him, he knew, even if Glenn wasn't a real friend, there'd only be disappointment. That evening he had stood up and moved to the men's room just to wash his hands, then slipped out to the parking lot without rejoining the table. Denise never sat next to him again, not until they were in his car now, she leaning against the passenger door, hands folded in her lap.

•

"Why are you all dolled up?" Peter asked her when they stopped for a red light.

She pulled the dress down over her knees. "I always like to make a good impression."

Though she was staring straight ahead, mouth fixed, he sensed that she was smirking. "We'll be driving from dawn till midnight," he said. "You won't meet anybody but gas jockeys, and you'll be too tired to show yourself off."

"Then you'll have to be the one to appreciate me."

"Why don't you pretend you've fixed yourself up for Glenn?"

"It wouldn't do me any good." She laughed. "Glenn knows all my secrets."

•

On the interstate, every time Peter pushed the Escort past seventy, he felt a hesitation, a surging in the engine, the car starting to vibrate, probably from bad alignment.

"Shit."

Denise looked up as if startled from a reverie. "Did you say something?"

"I said, shit. It's the goddamn car. We won't be able to go past 65."

"So?"

"We'll lose time."

"Does that matter?"

"We've only got two weeks. I don't want to waste most of it on the road."

"Who says we can't stay longer? As long as we like?"

"We have jobs. Remember?"

"Pull off at any exit and there are other jobs. No worse than what we're doing now."

"But our lives are back home." Peter found himself agitated, as if this were a real discussion and he had a point to prove.

"And what kind of life do you have there?"

"Not much. But it's the only one I've got."

"See? There's nothing to lose."

"But you have Glenn." Peter pictured Glenn pounding at his terminal, lanky, red-cheeked, fair-haired, with large knobby joints, as if he had been snapped together. He was always earnest, intent on doing good work.

"With Glenn," she said, "two weeks or two months or two years is no big deal."

"How do you mean?"

"I'd walk in the door, and he'd say, 'Oh, it's you.'"

•

"Tell me something," Peter asked her. "Were you really planning a trip before you heard about mine?"

Denise studied her fingers, bit at a split nail. "Of course not. But I have enough sense to seize an opportunity."

"What opportunity is that?"

21

"We have one car, and I can't afford air fare."

"You both work."

"Money never lasts with us."

For a second, Peter was about to ask her why, then suspected he wouldn't want to know the reason. Instead he said, "What will you do once we get there?" The plan was for him to drop her off at the rapid transit station in his old town, and she'd head into San Francisco, eventually get in touch with him to make arrangements for the drive back.

"Indulge my whims."

"Do you have friends there?"

"I have friends everywhere. It's very easy to make friends. Try it sometime."

"I know enough people," he said.

•

Midday they stopped fifteen minutes for sandwiches, gas, and a toilet break, then back on the road that barely changed for hours, a straight line of macadam cut through contoured fields out to the horizon, a blur of farmhouses and silos, acres of dried corn stalks, every now and then a town in the distance. Peter told Denise to turn on the radio, but all they could get were commodities quotes and ranting call-in shows. They listened to the slap of tires and the groan of the engine.

At dusk Denise took over the driving for the first time, spending several minutes adjusting the seat, making faces when she pulled back onto the highway. "Jesus, Peter, this transmission feels like tar."

"Sorry I couldn't offer more style."

"No matter. I'm a very flexible woman, able to shift my own gears."

•

When night fell and headlights cut into the darkness, Denise said, "What about sleeping?"

Peter held his watch to the dashboard. "We've got hours till midnight."

22

"I didn't mean that. What arrangements? One room or two."

He couldn't see the expression on her face. "Two, I suppose."

"There was a night a few months ago," she said, "when you could have gotten into my pants."

"I remember."

"But you weren't interested."

"No."

"You may have missed the window of opportunity." For a moment she was silent, then laughed out loud. Peter had never seen her so amused. "So," she continued, "your virtue is safe with me in one room. Besides, we'd save money."

"All right."

Later, after rehearsing the question in his mind for a half hour, the exact words to use, he asked her, "Why was the window unlocked that one time?"

"Curiosity. I wanted to find out if you're really as dull as you seem."

"All you had to do was ask. I'm probably the dullest person you know."

She laughed again. "Then think of all the effort we've saved ourselves. I got my answer without working up a sweat."

•

They pulled off the interstate the first exit they came to after midnight and found a motel right at the cloverleaf, a flat cinder block building with a neon sign thirty feet in the air. Peter paid for the room with his credit card, and Denise gave him cash for her half, counted out the bills before they left the car even though he told her there was no hurry. The room smelled of an earthy dampness, the walls slick to the touch.

Peter used the bathroom first, took a shower to be ready for a quick departure first thing in the morning. He was in and out in five minutes, then burrowed under the spread of one bed. But, tired as he was, he couldn't sleep, hearing Denise's sounds behind the bathroom door — clatterings on the glass shelf, the constant on and off of faucets, a flushing roar, something dropped on the tiles. It seemed she was in there for an hour.

When she came back into the room, Peter opened one eye from the pillow and saw her standing at the picture window in a long nightgown, her body outlined by the neon glow, the heavy shape of her legs, the contour of her small breasts. His arousal surprised him. It wasn't her, he told himself; it was being in a strange room with a strange woman. He rolled over and faced the wall, wanting no part of Denise.

•

When his alarm watched buzzed at 6 a.m., she was already dressed, in slacks and a fine knit sweater this time, heating water for the instant coffee left on a table by the door. He threw on his jeans and tee shirt, strapped the sandals. She pulled back the curtains to a grey morning, and they sat in plastic chairs drinking the thin, tepid coffee and eating stale rolls.

"Some fun," Denise said.

"I've been in worse places."

"With worse people?"

"I remember places better than people."

"You're kind of a place yourself."

"How do you mean?"

"A shape on the landscape. Something for the passersby to glance at and forget."

"Somebody who won't climb through a window if you opened it for him?"

"Exactly."

"Then it's a lucky thing you have Glenn."

"My luck is amazing."

•

The Escort wouldn't start, not after five minutes of twisting the key and grinding the starter. A few times the engine sputtered, but died as soon as Peter gave it gas. He beat fists on the steering wheel. "Goddamn it, goddamn it, goddamn it."

Denise covered his hand when he moved to turn the key again. "You'll wear down the battery. It's probably flooded. Let's just sit for a while."

He shook his head and winced. "What a goddamn way to live."

"What way?"

"A car like this piece of shit."

"It's not good to get so emotional about a machine."

"Oh yeah? How else are you going to get to San Francisco?"

"Something else would have come along."

"What?"

She gave a small shrug. "I'm not like you. When an obstacle arises, I trust my luck."

He wrenched the key so hard he thought it would snap. But the engine roared, spewed out a surge of thick, black exhaust.

•

Peter turned on the radio himself this time, dialed through the static crackle until he heard a voice, somebody reading from the Bible, a cadence filled with yeahs and verilies. He left it on even when a preacher's voice urged people to cast off their sinful ways. "Maybe we should pay attention," he said.

"You and me?" Denise laughed. "We're two people who resisted temptation. Think of all the goodness points we earned last night."

"I didn't think you kept track."

"It's not a bad idea to have an ace in the hole."

He turned the volume down to a meaningless hum in the speakers. "I'd have thought Glenn had stored up enough points from both of you."

"We must know different Glenns," she said.

"The one I know plays by the rules."

"Mine is working off demerits."

"From what?"

"He'll have to tell you that. One of my rules is never to talk about poor Glenn."

"Why are you here — off by yourself?"

"I didn't notice him stopping me."

"What kind of a marriage is that?"

"Ours."

•

At a gas station, they filled the tank and bought sandwiches and soda from a cooler, eating in the car, Denise driving now, touching a napkin to her lips after each bite and brushing crumbs from her sweater as soon as they fell. When a glob of mayonnaise dropped onto Peter's tee shirt, he saw her watching and deliberately left it there until she reached over and wiped it away.

"Your life needs a woman's touch," she said.

He looked at her and swallowed his anger, silently counting one to fifty, refusing to say anything.

"You've never been married." She continued as if he had responded. "You've probably never even asked anybody. You're the kind of person who lives in a room with all the shades pulled. Afraid you wouldn't know what to do if you saw something interesting out there. So it's better not to find out."

"No!" He snapped the denial.

Denise gave him a surprised look. "No what?"

"I asked somebody once." Peter felt his leg trembling and clamped both hands down on his knee.

"And?"

"She said yes."

"So?"

"It didn't work out." He stared out the window, far ahead, into a vague distance where he thought he saw the outline of mountains, dark shapes wavering out at the edge of his vision.

When he moved to turn the radio up, Denise pinched his fingers in hers and snapped it off.

"Time for you to tell me about your life," she told him.

26

"That's not something I talk about."

"It happened out where you're going, didn't it?"

He nodded.

"Are you trying to find her? Repair your past after years of regret?" Denise made her voice breathless: "Darling, it was all a terrible mistake."

"She's not there any more. I wouldn't be going back if she was."

"She broke your poor heart."

"I broke her jaw," he blurted, then reached out as if to snatch back the words.

"Whoa!" Denise let out a snort. "Silent Peter?"

"I got jealous. It's always been that way. Whenever there's a woman in my life, I get fierce with jealousy." He found it easy to speak now, as if finally revealing his shame had made it trivial, no worst than admitting he bit his nails.

"What happened?"

"We were at a party. Her friend's apartment. I got up for drinks and found her dancing with somebody else. All harmless, but I went wild. Dragged her outside, punched her, kept punching her until people pulled me away."

"Were you drunk?"

"No. I never get drunk. The way I am comes from inside me.

"What does?"

"Whenever I have anything, I get furious with myself because I expect to lose it."

Denise took her foot off the gas and turned toward Peter. "Would you hit me?"

"For what?"

"I don't know. Dancing with a stranger."

"Why would I? You're nobody to me."

●

By evening, the rock face of the mountains was closing in, as if just over the next rise of the foothills. But they drove another hour, Peter at the wheel, and didn't seem to get any nearer, though the inclines were steeper now. He was leaning forward on the seat, tensing his body, thinking the car would slide backwards if he relaxed.

"You're going to be this way for the rest of your life," Denise said. "Aren't you?"

"How's that?" He spoke through clenched teeth.

"Miserable."

They reached the crest and began an abrupt descent, picking up great speed, Peter taking his hands off the wheel, glancing at Denise for a reaction, waiting for her to cry out. But she sat with her hands folded, and he was the one to slam into a skid at the edge of a ditch.

Then uphill again, the Escort shuddered, sending jolts up through his legs. The metal seemed to be flapping with vibration, and their speed slowed no matter how hard he pressed the gas. He slammed the transmission into low gear and they crept upward, reaching the top just as a great rush of steam rushed from under the hood. "Fucking head gasket!" he cried.

Denise began laughing, first quietly, openmouthed, barely making a sound. Then she roared, arms wrapped around her middle, tears running down her face. "Oh, Peter! Nothing ever goes right for you!"

Ahead, as they coasted downhill, he saw the arch of a bridge, a great sweeping river that glittered in the sunset, and beyond a town, all white, a wonderland set against the mountains. He just steered, without power, moving from simple inertia, rumbling over the bridge onto the main street, where he turned against the curb before he lost all momentum.

•

They found the town's one hotel a block away, just four rooms on the second storey over a bar. Denise took her smallest suitcase from the trunk and Peter his dufflebag. He left her in the room to walk to a garage, where the one attendant, a kid working the gas pumps, told him the mechanic was gone for the day. He'd have to wait till morning.

When Peter got back, he saw Denise at a table in the bar talking to two men leaning forward on their stools, both in tapered jeans and cowboy boots, one with a wide brimmed felt hat and a mustache. She introduced him to the men, and he sat at the table with her, reported what the kid had said.

"If it's a gasket," the one with the mustache, Curtis, said, "they'll have to order the part. Could take days."

"It looks like we may have to change our plans," Denise said. Peter saw that she was smiling, as if they were acting out an elaborate joke.

"Plenty to do around here," Curtis told them. His friend Eddie nodded. Curtis signaled the bartender for more beers, one for Peter, another vodka martini for Denise.

Eddie offered Denise a cigarette, and she took it, rolling the filter on her thick, glossed lips. Peter had never seen her smoke, not for two long days in the car, not back home when she was with Glenn. Curtis snapped a flame from a polished silver lighter, and she drew in deeply, exhaling a stream of smoke in their faces.

Both Curtis and Eddie hooked boot heels over the rungs of their stools, swiveling back and forth, hovering over the table. Denise was talking to both of them, rattling on about nothing, but Peter could see her watching him out of the corner of her eye, awaiting his reaction. She moved her fingers away from her face, her jaw only inches from the arm he propped on the tabletop.

Peter stood at once. "I'll be back."

He thought Denise shook her head, once, abruptly, like a spasm. But he went up to the room and stretched out on the double bed, her suitcase open on one side, soft silk garments draped over the sides. He wouldn't touch anything.

After a half hour, Peter got up, pushed his tee shirt under his belt, and ran a hand through his hair. He was certain Denise would be gone when he got downstairs, her other two suitcases missing from his useless car, already miles from this town with a stranger who was now her friend. He wondered which man he would find left at the bar, Curtis or Eddie, maybe neither.

For a moment he thought he might stay in this town. Forever. Or until something happened. But he knew when his car was finally fixed, he would turn around and go back home, spending the days on the road wondering what he and Glenn would talk about when he got there.

Escaping This Place

"**I** hate it here!" Francoise spat the words at Mark.

He was carrying a bag of groceries across the cinder driveway to his apartment and she was hanging clothes in a corner of the yard. She tugged a pair of Nicole's jeans from the basket and flung them over the rope line. Mark cringed at the pulley's squeal.

"This place — it is terrible."

Her accent was hoarse and liquid. She couldn't speak a sentence without rolling her eyes and gesticulating.

Mark had always imagined French women petite, with delicate cheekbones and long, lean noses. But Francoise, the first he had ever known, was large and florid, her calves thick, her arms muscled, her face crowded with oversized features. He couldn't understand what had appealed to Connor, why the man had bothered to bring her across an ocean as a wife. But he felt sorry for her, for the mess of her divorce, and offered himself as an appeasing listener, this time propped his grocery sack against the side of the house to hear another repetition of her lament.

"What kind of judges do you have in this country?" Francoise threw up her hands. "Your Judge Yoder refuses to allow my children to visit their mother's home. Because that bastard of a father protests. They regard me as the guilty one because I am a foreigner. What disgusting laws you have here."

"We're kind of provincial in this state," Mark said.

She pondered frowning. "How does this mean — provincial?"

"Narrow-minded. We think every place else is wrong because it's not like us."

"I just want the children to see their grandmere and grandpere. And your judge — your Yoder — he says my parents should come to here. I wouldn't insult my parents by bringing them to such a country."

Francoise treated Mark as an ally, seeming to forget that he was a native who had rarely left the town, that he even worked for the county, sifting documents for the Department of Roads.

Her conversation was a broken record — the crimes of Connor, the imbecility of Judge Yoder, the gross ignorance of Americans, the ugliness of the landscape. Still he heard her out because it fascinated him that this woman devoted so much hatred to the only place he had known in his twenty-seven years.

Mark stood an inch shorter than Francoise, and where her bigness seemed substantial, the skin taut on her arms and legs, he felt slack and overweight, flabby in the middle, embarrassed by the width of his trousers.

He walked with an awkward limp, the left foot deformed at birth, now roughly shaped after a dozen operations. At work every time he passed the secretaries to move from his cubicle to the file room, his lurching gait made him redden. But Francoise never appeared to notice, so absorbed was she in the calamity that had taken her from France.

Her daughter Nicole did. He could see the girl's troubled eyes whenever he approached. She was the most serious six-year-old he had ever known, brow perpetually furrowed under a pile of brown hair that her mother brushed a hundred strokes each evening. Gerard, the son, eight, long gangly legs protruding from short pants, was always running, playing games in the reaches of the neighborhood far past sunset, until Francoise had to stand at her door and shout his name.

Nicole never strayed far from her mother. She appeared from the apartment now, carrying wet doll dresses that, without a word, she handed Francoise to hang beside her wash. She edged behind her mother's broad hip, shying away from Mark. If he had not been there, she would have spoken. In fact, she chattered constantly when she thought she was alone with Francoise. On weekends, when his windows were open, Mark could hear the perpetual singsong of her high little voice.

Francoise pulled shirts and pants from the laundry basket, her own substantial underwear, slapping each garment across the line. "I'm a prisoner," she said, reaching down to touch a hand to Nicole's fluffy hair. "My children are prisoners."

Mark nodded, half wishing that he had never met her, had never learned a person could feel so trapped.

•

For all Francoise's lamenting, Mark had few clear facts of her situation. Connor, then an army sergeant stationed in Germany, met her on a week-long holiday in the south of France, part of a crowd constantly opening wine bottles and shouting laughter, her brain floating the whole time. One evening he seduced her while she lay numb and giggling. She became pregnant with Gerard, Connor took leave from Germany to marry her in her village church, and when his duty tour was up he brought her back to the States, to this town that she hated. Their marriage was a ceaseless quarrel, with a long enough truce to conceive Nicole. But by the time the baby was born, Connor was hitting her. She found the apartment, and one day when Connor was at work, moved the children, their beds and clothing. Mark remembered their arrival, the big woman hoisting mattresses from the roof of her car. He offered to help and had been her confidant ever since, so attuned to her grievances that he could sense nuances of each French curse.

•

A century ago their house had belonged to the owner of a successful farm, acres of rich black soil thick with rye plants during each summer's flourishing. But the town had grown up around it, eating away at land too valuable for crops. Finally, the house was divided into five apartments, two on each storey and Mark's on the bottom level dug into a knoll of earth. He rented three small rooms with a door at the back and narrow, welled windows on one side.

Francoise and her children lived directly above. He could hear their footsteps, the closing of doors, the rush of water. Except for the hours she worked, she was rarely away from home. Mark knew because he was there as much, watching television or reading paperback adventures.

Right after dinner every night, Francoise gave Nicole and Gerard their French lesson. If he sat in the bedroom under hers and opened the window, Mark could hear the murmur of their sounds. Once he considered buying a cassette course in the language to give himself a hobby, imagining the expression on Francoise's face when he spoke to her in her native tongue. But he would have felt like a fool making the purchase in a store where they knew him.

•

Mark had been born to elderly parents who never could get used to the child that had intruded into their long dry marriage. His father ran a small farm on the town's outskirts, a man much better with mechanical objects than with crops. His mother always seemed to be standing at the kitchen stove, cooking and preserving, the old wooden house moist with the steam of boiling.

The deformed foot obsessed both his parents, the fact about him that convinced them their son was real. Even though he had been very small at the time, Mark could remember the doctor telling his mother that she should count her blessings there was no worse consequence of a pregnancy at her age. His father was always running callused fingertips over the odd angles of the bones, as if they were a problem he should be able to fix.

In school, even though Mark could play no sports, was the one assigned to keep score on the sidelines, no one teased him. People had never said anything, but he could feel their eyes uneasy behind a polite indifference.

His parents died when Mark was twenty, the farm in so much debt that structures and land and implements were all auctioned by the bank. Now a warehouse with a corrugated roof covered the area where the house and barn had stood, a parking lot much of the fields.

The few friends of his school years still lived in the area. They spoke briefly when they met him in stores, wives at their sides, children tugging their hands. Three years ago he had dated briefly, a pale, freckled girl from a county office as scrawny as he was overweight. They went to movies together and ate in restaurants that left the smell of grease in his hair. She seemed a sad girl, but now and then he said something that made her face light up with a smile. There wasn't a second they spent together that he didn't feel nervous. Yet alone in the darkness of his room he thought he loved her. One night he found the courage to clutch her for a few quick kisses, unable to speak his feelings. Then he worried that all her responses, from the time she accepted his stammered offer of a date, might have their source in pity. He became afraid to call her again, and she took a job somewhere else.

•

Francoise stormed from the porch to his car the moment he pulled into the drive. From her face, the burning cheeks, the fixed unblinking eyes, Mark knew he would hear that Connor had done something terrible again.

She exploded the second she saw him. "That bastard! He's having me in court again. He calls me an unfit mother. Me!"

"For what? He's the one behind in his child support."

"He accuses me. He says I teach the children not to love their country."

"That's crazy," he said, at once sensing the inadequacy of his words.

"This country is a sewer!" She gripped the door handle so hard Mark thought her knuckles would burst through the skin.

•

The next time they spoke, two days later, Francoise met him at the back doorway and thrust a paper in his face.

"What's this?" Mark said.

"From your court. From your Judge Yoder. A restraining order!

I am not allowed to take the children out of the county without first seeking his permission." Her thick arms quivered with the force of her anger.

"The county? Does he have the right?"

"He is your judge. He can do anything he wishes. There is no justice in this place."

"But why should he do that?" Mark immediately shared her agitation.

"He accuses me. He says I plan to abduct the children."

"Abduct them? Where?"

"To France!"

"But you only want to visit."

"I am not allowed to visit. I can do nothing." She threw up her hands. "I am not allowed to breathe without the approval of your Judge Yoder."

"Don't listen to him. He's treating you like a prisoner." Mark heard himself shouting, his voice as loud as Francoise's, his cheeks flushed.

"If I try, he will take my children!" Her face collapsed and he expected howls of rage, but she realigned her features with a snap of her head. "He will deny me the custody of them and send them to live with that Connor."

"Can't you fight it? What about your lawyer?"

"My lawyer is a puppy. Your Judge Yoder barks and he runs with his tail between his legs."

"I've never heard of anything so unfair. Why is life so unfair?" Mark's muscles were quivering, his clenched fists pounding his thighs. "You have to do something."

"What? Tell me what you would do?"

"Escape. Get away from here as far and as fast as I could."

Francoise seized his arm, brought her face close to his, and spoke in a hoarse whisper. "Would you help me do that?"

"You have to fight." His head was swirling, a great sinking in his middle, as he realized what he was saying.

•

At his work, Mark felt people were staring at him for acting so strangely. He couldn't make himself pay attention to the papers, constantly looking up and meeting someone's eyes. Once when he had to go to a file cabinet, he forgot to concentrate on his walking, the unbalance of each step. His leg twisted under him and he crashed into a table spread with forms, jarring them to the floor, gripping an edge for support while secretaries sprang from their chairs to help him.

"I'm all right," he insisted, "I'm all right," fearing what they would say if they knew of his promise to help Francoise flee.

•

Just past ten, Francoise tapped three times on the water pipes in her kitchen and the metal clanged in Mark's apartment. He opened his door and slowly climbed the stairs, ready to hurry back down if a neighbor appeared. That was Francoise's idea. She did not want anyone to know that they were meeting. She didn't trust the town, sure her every movement was reported back to Connor.

He scratched a fingernail on her door and she quickly pulled him inside. "They're finally asleep. Speak softly. They mustn't know."

"Till when?"

"We won't be safe till the airplane is off the ground." She stood close to him, her breath heavy on his cheek.

Mark sighed and gripped a chair. "What should I do?"

"They are following me. I am permitted to do nothing. Every time if I drive in the car with Nicole and Gerard to any place but my work, someone tells Connor and he calls the police. So you must do everything."

"Whatever you want."

"You know every road, every way out of this place. It is your job. You must be the driver to get us away."

He nodded.

"And you must buy the tickets. But not in this town. If you buy for one adult and two children, someone will understand and tell your Judge Yoder."

"I'll go to the city. Take a vacation day."

She gripped his arm. "And another to get me to the airplane."

"As many as you need." His blood was pounding.

"I will leave everything behind as if we stay." She indicated the possessions of the apartment with a sweeping hand gesture. "But we must have clothing to wear, my children and I."

"I'll buy you clothes," he offered.

"No. That is not necessary. This is what we will do. I will wash clothing and hang it to dry. You will take down pieces when no one looks. Not all. Just some things. You will lock the clothing in your car in paper sacks. Later we will buy suitcases in the airport."

"You've planned it all so carefully," he said.

"I have thought of nothing but escape since the day I arrived in this place."

•

They became public friends when Francoise decided it was necessary for her strategy. She wanted people used to seeing them together, she and the children in his car. "There will be so many reports about us that your Judge Yoder will have to throw up his hands."

Mark was invited for dinner, wearing tie and jacket, sitting at the table in uncomfortable formality with Gerard and Nicole looking down at their plates, only Francoise talking, serving, pouring wine. Mark had heard so much about French cuisine that he was eager for the first meal. But Francoise cooked badly, the vegetables limp, the meat chewy, the sauces thick and clotted.

They went on a picnic, the four of them in Mark's car, with a cooler of food he bought at the supermarket. In the park Nicole ran with her brother, chasing rabbits, fascinated by the groundhogs that popped from the ground, giggling and screaming, hiding and suddenly appearing to throw their arms around Francoise's neck and then darting off again.

Mark envied her the love of her children, and she spoke for hours of how wonderful they were, their grades in school, their progress with their true language.

As much as he wanted Francoise's plan to succeed, he found himself wishing he could watch these children grow up and see what would become of their lives in this town.

•

Mark heard angry voices from Francoise's apartment, a man shouting, Francoise's harsh curses. He paced for ten minutes, unsure what to do. Should he go up? Should he get help? He went out into the yard, around the side of the house, until he could see the shadows of two figures outlined behind the curtains. They were moving constantly back and forth in the room, but apart. If he saw the man's shape close in on her, if he saw an arm raised, he would cry out for the neighbors. Then he heard a door slam and watched a man stomp toward a car parked at the curb. The engine roared, thick smoke poured from the exhaust, the car jolted away on squealing tires.

At once Mark rushed back inside and dialed Francoise's number. She picked up at the first ring, spoke without bothering with a greeting, knowing it was he. "That bastard! He wanted to have the children in the middle of the week. That's not for his visiting. I made them to hide in their rooms. Nothing will make me happier than to know he will never see them again."

When she hung up, Mark thought about Connor for the first time, a man he had heard damned for months, now a shape in the darkness. His first reaction was that the man was being deprived of his son and daughter. Then he realized he didn't care. Nothing mattered but winning — he and Francoise over Connor and the community. If their plan hadn't been at stake, he would have shouted his elation.

•

"Soon," Francoise said every time they met, hissing the word. "It must be soon." Her arms had broken out into a rash; her face was splotched.

Within the week Mark took his vacation day and drove the five hours to the city to buy the tickets. He laid out the money because Francoise did not want to make such a noticeable withdrawal from her account. She was sure the bank would report it to Judge Yoder.

Past midnight on the last night, Nicole left three small bags outside his door, toothbrushes, medicines, the children's favorite toys. He waited until all the lights in the house were out, the building absolutely quiet, before loading them into his trunk.

An hour from dawn the water pipe clanged once. He sat up immediately on the couch where he had been unable to sleep, listening to his heart beat in the darkness. For weeks he thought he would be frightened when the time came. But now his mind felt crystal with alertness.

Gerard left the house first, crouching in the shadows and then darting to the parking area to climb into the back seat of Mark's unlocked car. A few minutes later, Nicole. She moved much more slowly than her brother, pausing to look back at the window where her mother stood, confused by this game Francoise had told her they were playing. Why were they starting for this picnic in the darkness? Why wasn't anyone allowed to know?

Mark hobbled out next, trying to hurry, afraid his leg would give way and send him thudding to the ground, waking neighbors, a dozen faces at the windows. When he made it to the driver's seat, his sweat-drenched body shivered in the morning chill. He crouched low and faced the children with a finger to his lips.

Francoise came last, stepping quickly for such a large woman. Mark pinched his finger on the ignition key, ready to twist. But she paused beside the car to stare back at the house, at the trees, and the grey yard around them. Then she got inside.

"What is it?" he said, certain something was wrong.

"I want to remember every inch of this place. I want never to forget what I've despised so much."

•

Mark backed slowly from his parking spot and then crept out of the driveway, conscious of the tires crunching gravel. On the street he drove cautiously, taking a tortuous route so that anyone who saw the car would not realize it was heading for the highway. But he only stayed on the highway for a quarter mile, turning onto the first dirt county road they came to. He didn't need a map after all the days of staring at county road plans, memorizing the network of intersections.

Nicole and Gerard curled dozing on the back seat. Francoise sat beside him with her eyes closed as if in prayer, clenching her fists against her thighs.

With the sunrise the children woke and sat up, asking dozens of questions. Where were they? Why were they going this way? When would they get to the picnic? Would there be animals?

"Wait and see," was all Francoise would say. The children were hungry. They began to whine. But their mother would not stop for breakfast. "Later," she told them. "When we get there."

Mark had known this landscape all his life. It had been as much a part of him as his twisted foot. But now, for the first time, he saw it as a stranger: flat to the horizon, caked brown soil, endless acres of rustling corn husks, black crows scattering from the road as the car bore down.

He broke the silence to tell her when they had crossed the county line. Tears ran down her face. "Now hurry!" she urged. "Drive as fast as you can."

Francoise appeared to stay calm, but Mark expected sirens, flashing lights, a roadblock ahead, Judge Yoder in his black robes, Connor in his military uniform aiming a rifle.

Nicole clutched her stomach and twisted on the seat. "I'm so hungry, Mama." She began to cry, and Francoise snapped on the radio, turned it so loud the speakers vibrated.

For a half hour they had to creep behind a truck on a twisting two lane road with continual no passing zones. But by mid-morning they had left the state and were only an hour from the airport outside the city. The traffic was becoming thicker, the road lined with stores.

Francoise made him stop when she saw a display of suitcases. "They will be cheaper here," she said. She came back with three folded blue nylon bags and candy bars for the children. Mark took the sacks of clothing from the trunk, and while he drove the rest of the way, the three of them refolded garments and packed them properly. Francoise made a game of it, singing the French names of each one — chemise, pantalon, jupe. The children asked no questions. Mark wondered if they realized they were about to leave the only life they had ever known.

•

At the airport, Mark got their boarding passes and checked the new blue bags. He bought Nicole and Gerard breakfast. Francoise wanted only coffee, and he had no appetite. They sat listening to the children's memories of yesterday's television cartoons, a cat pulverized into dust, a duck hollowed by a cannon ball, creatures who marvelously sprang back to wholeness. He wasn't sure what to say to Francoise. The important subjects could not be mentioned with the children here: What will you do? Where will you live? Have you told your family?

A voice announced their flight. Mark walked with them to the gate. When he passed through the metal detector, he finally believed they had defeated Connor and Judge Yoder, triumphed over the entire town.

At the gate, where he could go no further, Francoise turned and shook his hand. "I will send you the money for the tickets."

It doesn't matter, he wanted to say: we've won! His face opened with a smile and he stepped forward to embrace her. But she was gone, halfway down the ramp, a large, bulky woman with a child gripping each hand.

Mark waited for the plane to take off, the only person left at the gate by the time it taxied out and queued on the runway. He stood against the window, watching the acres of tarmac through his reflection in the glass. Finally, their plane took its turn, lifting off the ground with a great roar of jets. Its silver body glinted as it banked and soared upward toward the cloud cover. He moved from window to window to follow its path, then stepped outside, his head bent back as far as it would go when the plane disappeared.

Homemaking

Harold talked them into moving. He was Steve and Debra's successful friend, full of advice for Steve since they were college freshman a dozen years ago. But Steve, bored and broke, had dropped out as a first semester sophomore, didn't even bother to buy textbooks, relieved to find a job servicing machines in a shipping department. Harold went on to a business degree, a career as a marketing manger, and a four-bedroom colonial in an upscale subdivision. So at first Steve and Debra didn't take him seriously when he argued that they should rent a house. Of course, they agreed the apartment was much too small, cramped, just two rooms. But how could they afford a bigger place?

A brown metal unit with a two-burner stove, sink, and cube refrigerator took up the back wall of the room where they ate and watched TV from a sagging sofa wedged against a playpen piled with toys and stuffed animals. In the other room, a plaid spread on a clothesline separated their bed from Molly's crib. Half their clothes wouldn't fit into the one narrow closet and had to be stored in cardboard boxes crammed under the box spring. When Harold pointed at the clutter and shook his head, Steve just sighed.

Though they lived at opposite ends of the same town, Harold didn't contact them for months at a time, then all of a sudden would be around constantly, he and his wife, Cheryl, coming by several times a week with bottles of French wine, sometimes calling first, sometimes just showing up. Harold was a big man, freckled and red-faced, curly haired, overweight, noisily enthusiastic, half shouting when he spoke. Cheryl, small and taut, sharp nosed, said very little, her eyes intense, as if keeping secrets.

Steve just wanted to chew over old times when they visited —

boom boxes blasting from the dorm roof, water balloons dropped from windows, the night they raced cars on the stadium track. But Harold went on and on about the apartment, pointing out the ironing board leaning against a corner, the pots hanging from a wall, the chipped enamel table, the coats heaped on the rack by the door. "This is no way for you and Debra to live. Not with a kid." He said it every time, pointing to Molly's crib with his eyes raised, though — childless himself — he never picked her up. Debra would look to Cheryl with a silent appeal, but Cheryl seemed oblivious, savoring a juice glass of Bordeaux, her gaze fixed on the lights reflected in the window.

Certainly, Debra would tell Harold, they wanted to move, desperately, but money was the problem. They were barely breaking even. Still, the more Harold went on, the more Steve wavered, half believing he could figure out a way to manage a higher rent. But Debra would say, "We can't afford it," each time after Harold left, fingers trembling as she calculated and recalculated their budget, copying rows of numbers onto a small lined pad.

Then Debra became pregnant again, probably the Saturday Harold and Cheryl stayed till 3 and left an open bottle for her and Steve to finish. They had fallen into a groggy lovemaking, too bleary-eyed in the morning to remember if they had taken precautions. They hadn't, and now Steve could imagine no logistical possibilities for coping with another baby in the two rooms. Debra suggested putting their bed in the living area and getting rid of the sofa; the springs were dragging on the floor anyway. But when he said, "Do you really want to live like that?" she shook her head and wept.

•

So they house hunted, Steve mostly, following up listings Harold tore from the newspaper, ragged-edged slips of paper he would stuff into Steve's shirt pocket. When Steve found one he liked, he went back with Debra, who toted year-old Molly in a back pouch and fingered the calculator in her purse, convincing him that the rent was hundreds too much.

"Maybe I can get a better job," Steve said.

"In this town?" Debra gave a hopeless shrug. "In this world? What can you do?"

He knew she was right, but resented her saying it, as if the economy were his fault. "I'm good with my hands. When I quit college, I started off making good money."

"Hands don't matter any more. You should have stayed in school."

Her words were flat, a statement of fact, not an accusation, but Steve felt his face burning. He tried to turn it into a joke. "Too much partying with Harold."

"Harold graduated."

Steve looked away from her, unwilling to meet her eyes. "Harold's smart."

"He didn't stop you from dropping out."

"It was me. I didn't want to be there."

"Why don't they ever invite us to their house?"

He'd never thought about it. Harold had always been like that, just showing up in his room the few nights he tried to study, looming in his doorway, oversized, too soft to be an athlete, suddenly challenging him to arm wrestle, always winning and then taking him out for beer and pizza. "It saves us a sitter."

"Is that what he said?"

"Harold's thoughtful."

"Then why doesn't he give you a job?"

Steve forced a laugh. "What can I do that he needs?"

•

Harold found them a house, bursting in with Cheryl while Steve and Debra were eating dinner, the apartment thick with hamburger sizzle. Harold looked very pleased with himself. On a whim, he told them, he had turned into a street that afternoon and saw the For Rent sign, wrote down the phone number of the real estate firm.

"And guess who the agent is?" Harold said.

Steve shook his head. He knew nothing about real estate.

"Old Martha Selig."

Debra winced. "The lady the pigs attacked?"

Cheryl nodded. Harold grinned. "The very one."

It seemed everyone in town knew the story, at least rumors about it. Steve remembered as Harold went on; he just hadn't associated the name. The attack happened many years ago, before he and Debra were even born. Now Martha Selig was a middle-aged woman. Then she had been a five-year-old feeding the pigs on her parents' farm several miles out in the country, dragging buckets of slops from the barn. The animals all knew her, crowding around grunting and snorting when she appeared in the afternoon. One day a sow just went berserk and set the others off. They swarmed Martha, trampled her with hooves, sank teeth into her flesh. She spent three months in the hospital, a year in bed, walked with a cane ever since. People said she had terrible scars, lived in constant pain.

"Do we have to get a house from somebody like that?" Debra asked.

The others looked at her. "Somebody like what?" Cheryl asked.

"Maimed."

"You can't notice anything wrong with her except for the limp," Harold told her. "The pigs didn't get her face."

Debra sucked in her cheeks, as if fighting back morning sickness. Steve turned away.

Harold focused on Steve. "Listen. The rent isn't much more than this place. It's got two rooms downstairs and two up. You can afford it."

"What's the catch?" Steve said.

"It's small and old and needs lots of fixing."

"I think it's cute," Cheryl said.

"Would you want to live there?" Debra asked her.

"Sure. If I had no other choice."

•

Debra insisted that Steve check out the house by himself. "I don't want to see that woman."

"It wasn't her fault," he said. "Blame the pigs."

Debra shivered.

"You heard what Harold said. We can fix it up."

"Why do you always let Harold tell you what to do?"

"If I listened to you, we'd rot in this place." He squeezed fists, stifling anger.

"Harold doesn't know everything."

"He wants to help us."

"Who says we need it? Who says we need him?" Her eyes were moist, lips trembling. The pregnancy was growing, a swelling in the baggy jeans that made her look misshapen.

"It's not like we're doing so good on our own."

•

Steve met Martha Selig at her office and rode in her Buick to look at the house. She moved slowly and stiffly, emitted deep sighs getting in and out of the driver's seat; that was the only sign of her ordeal. But she wore dark slacks and long sleeves on a warm day, her top buttoned high on her neck. In the car Steve had expected the woman to feign good cheer and rattle on about the house. Instead she was dour and taciturn, as if annoyed that a client had disturbed her day.

Perhaps it was the property she was showing, a house with a rent that wouldn't bring her much of a commission. She took Steve out to a narrow half-paved street he hadn't known existed, where most of the homes were trailers packed one next to the other on bare cinder blocks. The house with the sign was the only two-story building on the block, very old, the flaked paint grey with soot, shutters missing, masking tape across cracks in the windows. An incongruous door in the middle of the second story opened out to a slanted porch roof too narrow to stand on.

When asked about it, Martha, as if begrudging the information, told him the house was historical, one of the first in the town, built by early settlers, originally centered on acres of farmland. It had been designed for Indian raids, she said, so people could hide upstairs and the savages couldn't rush up the narrow stairway. The odd door allowed for hoisting furniture onto the second floor.

"How long has it been empty?"

"A year." She paused. "Maybe two."

Inside someone had started ripping wallpaper from the parlor, not working systematically, leaving swaths of bare plaster on all four walls, dried strips with faded flowers hanging loose where wall met ceiling. The warped floorboards of the two front rooms were coated with peeling brown paint, the kitchen linoleum worn down to patches of felt backing. The cabinet doors all hung open, the shelves lined with yellowed newspaper. Only the gas stove was new, gleaming white. The owner, Martha explained, got it on sale when he refurbished two of his other properties.

"Why didn't he fix this one up?" Steve wondered.

"It wouldn't be worth it. He'd have to charge the same rent as houses in the good part of town, and who'd want to live here if they could afford there?"

•

Back in the apartment, Steve wasn't sure. The more he described the house to Debra the more uncertain he became. "There's a narrow stairs to the second floor behind a door that looks like a coat closet. You have to duck your head and edge up sideways."

"It sounds," Debra said, biting her lips, drawing in her face, "much worse than here." He wanted to tell her to stop, that she was making herself ugly.

Then Harold showed up, eager, pushing a laundry basket aside as he sprawled on the sofa. "So what's it like inside?" He made Steve go through the details all over again. "Everything you're telling me is cosmetic. A scrubbing, a few panes of glass, a coat of paint. It's four rooms, a real kitchen, space for two kids. Debra's due in a couple of months." He pointed to the bulge of her pregnancy. "You'd be crazy not to take it."

"When am I supposed to get all this painting and fixing up done?"

"We'll find help," Harold promised, emphatic. "Get everybody we know to put in, say, two hours scraping and painting. One weekend and the place will be sparkling."

After Harold left, Debra buried her head in the sofa's padding and hugged her knees to her chest. "I don't want to move."

"You won't have to do a thing." Steve kicked aside the laundry and stood over her. "We'll take care of it all."

She gave him a bleary look, face ashen, than ran into the bathroom and dropped in front of the toilet.

•

Harold's weekend turned out to be closer to a month. Late in the evenings, working under dim ceiling bulbs, Steve hoped the need for a second coat wouldn't be so obvious after the paint dried. A few friends did help, mainly people Harold knew, at least the first days, then they ended up having other commitments. Even Harold kept having to work late, calling at the last minute to cancel, promising to make up the time.

One night when Steve was alone, standing in the middle of the floor and cursing at cracks too deep for spackle, a woman appeared, a shape in the darkness tapping at the warped screen door. Steve let her in, blushing, certain she had heard his obscenities.

"Harold sent me," she said when she introduced herself as Julia. Her head was covered by red bandana, her body wrapped in an oversize flannel shirt. "Lot's of work here," she said, then went up to the second floor with a paint can and a plastic drop cloth as if she knew exactly what had to be done. She painted so quietly that Steve shouted to ask if she was okay. "I'm great," she called down. When Julia left, he saw that she had finished a whole room.

The next night she arrived soon after Steve. He felt embarrassed that she was doing so much, a stranger putting aside her own life to help his. But she told him it gave her great enjoyment. "It's therapy. Taking part in a transformation. Helping to make something better."

At first, Steve found her a plain woman, long-faced and wide-hipped, too thin every place else. Then he came to like her energy, the snap of her dark eyes, the constant fluttering of her fingers when she talked. Working in the empty house, he spreading a broad path with the roller, Julia edging the trim with a narrow brush, her presence seemed a natural part of his day.

One evening Harold rushed in to check their progress, his car idling at the curb. He hurried from room to room and told them, "You two are doing a great job." He slapped Steve's shoulder, gave Julia a quick hug. Then he was gone. His visit couldn't have lasted more than two minutes.

Julia was laughing. "That's typical Harold."

"How well do you know him?"

"Oh, we're great friends."

"He never mentioned you before."

"He told me all about you." She reached out to touch his arm.

"College days?" He waited, apprehensive, realizing that he didn't want her to know what a fool he had been.

"About now."

"Money's always been tough for me."

"Harold wants you to be happy."

He set the roller down in the pan, wiped his hands across his shirtfront. "What about you? Does he want to make you happy too?" It struck him that he really cared to know.

"My life's fine. Ed's a good father. He takes care of our sons while I'm out with a paint brush trying to improve the world."

"When will I meet Ed?"

"Unlikely." Julia's smile surprised him. "We don't have the same friends."

"Not even Harold."

She shook her head.

"Doesn't that complicate your lives?"

"It makes things interesting."

They had started from different ends of the room, but met in the same corner. Julia dabbed at the molding, Steve smeared the roller near a light switch. Their arms touched as they worked. He put the roller down and closed his hand over hers, guiding her strokes. Then they stood together looking at the wall. "We're doing good work," Julia said.

He made himself step away from her.

•

Steve drove the rental truck for the move, uneasy at the wide yellow bulk behind him, the shrunken reflections in the side mirrors. Harold followed in his car with three friends Steve had never met before, all Harold's size, ex-athletes who had become beefy men, turning Steve's moving into a sport. Showing off their strength, they stood on the cab of the truck and single-handedly hoisted chests and mattresses up through the door on the porch roof. Ignoring Steve, they swigged from six packs of beer and called out challenges to each other.

Harold gave directions, a beer can in one hand, a sandwich in the other, shouting at the men, telling them where to put things. He was as big as they were, but looser, flabby in the middle.

The whole time, Steve kept pausing to look for Julia, wondering if she would come, how he would introduce her to Debra, what the two women would say to each other.

"Did you invite her to help?" he finally asked Harold when they had a moment alone.

"That should be up to you by now," Harold told him.

Debra came with Molly in Cheryl's car after all the furniture was inside, bringing two suitcases of clothing and leftover food from the apartment's kitchen. Molly toddled to the middle of the living room and sat on the bare floor with an expression of distress.

After he returned from driving the other men back, Harold flopped on the sofa and closed his eyes, even though he had done little lifting. He told Steve where he could find the good wine in Cheryl's trunk.

When Steve came back into the house, Debra was embracing Cheryl, a head taller, hair tangled, her pregnancy a barrier between them. Molly clung to her Debra's leg, lips trembling at the edge of tears, as if imitating her mother. Steve could see Cheryl was uncomfortable with the hug.

"Debra thinks the house looks empty," she told him as she pulled away and smoothed her jacket.

Debra blew her nose and nodded. "We don't have enough furniture."

"No problem," Harold said. "There's a farm auction next Saturday. Somebody died, left a house full of stuff."

•

When Debra told him she wouldn't go, that she had too much unpacking left, Steve didn't protest even though all she had done in the days since the move was sit at the kitchen table with a mug of coffee and stare at the stacked boxes. At work, on a break, he called Julia from a pay phone, swallowed when he heard her voice, then told her about the auction, adding that Harold would be there.

"It's always a treat to see Harold," she said and laughed as if sharing a joke.

The morning of the auction Steve and Harold met Julia in a downtown parking lot. She had borrowed her husband's van to bring back any furniture Steve was able to buy. Cheryl, Harold told them, had stayed behind to alter some of her old curtains for the downstairs windows.

Steve watched Harold and Julia closely, eager to see their interaction, wondering how they had ever become friends. But they said little to each other beyond polite greetings, Harold unusually quiet. He and Julia sat at opposite ends of the bench seat, Steve in the middle.

Even though farmland surrounded the town, Steve rarely went into the country. Any trips he took were on the interstate to the city several hours away, traveling so fast the view was a blur of corn stalks, cattle, and silos. But Julia knew the way right to the driveway of the farm having the auction. "I like to read maps," she explained, "to master new territory."

Implements were spread out on the gravel in front of the barn, domestic objects on metal folding tables close to the house — sets of mismatched china, table lamps, figurines, preserving jars with rubber seals, piles of old magazines, blankets heavy with mothballs.

"I wonder," Steve said, knowing the possibility was slight, "if this is the farm where the pigs mauled Martha Selig." Though the pens behind the barn were empty, he imagined the frantic stampede of the animals, mad squealing, grunts and snorts, a wild thrashing, teeth bared, the child's horrified shrieks. And for a moment he didn't want to own anything from this place.

"A different farm," Harold said, absolutely certain.

"What's wrong?" Julia asked Steve when Harold walked off to inspect a bureau.

"She must have thought feeding the pigs was routine. Then in a split second her world turned savage and nothing was ever the same again."

"Chance," Julia said. "If Harold hadn't turned a corner, you wouldn't have the house."

"Martha ended up with a life of pain, and we painted rooms together."

"Some of us turn out luckier than others." Julia touched his wrist with a fingertip.

Harold told Steve not to buy anything till late in the afternoon, when most people had left after spending their money and the bidding would go down. Some of the living room pieces, chairs and cabinets, were still available, and Steve owned them for a token payment, the auctioneer eager to end his day.

"So now you've got a full house," Harold slapped the side of the van when it was loaded. "Furniture, fresh paint, room to spread out."

"I told him some people have real luck." Julia smiled.

•

Back in town, Julia asked Harold to take over the driving and drop her by the stores. She had shopping to do. He could leave the van in the parking lot after they were finished. Let me stay with you, Steve wanted to ask her, then realized how impossible that would be.

Cheryl was gone when they reached the house, curtains in all the windows. Steve wondered what Harold would say if Debra asked where the van came from. But she just stood inside the doorway and watched them carry the furniture from the curb to the living room.

When Harold left, Debra told Steve that she didn't like having somebody else's belongings. "Why did those people sell?" she wanted to know.

"The old woman died," he explained. "A widow. There wasn't anyone left to take over the farm."

"Then all this"— she pointed at the chairs and cabinets and tables — "is like living with tombstones."

"That's crazy," he protested.

·

The baby was a boy, Timothy. The first snow of winter fell while Debra was in the hospital. Molly was staying with a friend of Cheryl's, and Steve drove home in the evening seeing his moonlit house surrounded by a still whiteness. Alone in the silent rooms, all the lamps off, he sat among the dark shapes of unfamiliar possessions, unwilling to climb the stairs.

Soon after he set up a second crib and brought the baby home, the temperature dropped far below freezing. Harold came by to report predictions of an unusually cold winter. The bedrooms were chilly, the forced air system weak; the fan wasn't sending heat up to the second floor. The thermometer Steve bought for upstairs didn't rise above 45 degrees. Debra took Timothy into their bed and piled five blankets on Molly.

Before he went to work the third frigid morning, Steve dialed Martha Selig's office and started to explain the problem. But before he could finish Debra started shouting from across the room, "I have babies, a newborn. This house is a health hazard!" Then she stood in sudden silence, her hands at her mouth. "My wife is very upset," Steve said, and Martha, flat and abrupt, told him she would send a repairman that evening.

The man, Everett, appeared long past dark, standing on the front porch in a greasy wool jacket, heavy work gloves, and a cap with earflaps pulled low on his face. He gave off the odor of heating oil. Steve followed him down to the basement, where they had to stoop to walk. The walls were rough stone, the floor just packed earth, the furnace propped up on bricks in the middle under a dim bulb that dangled from a joist. Steve took a deep breath of mold and immediately erupted in loud sneezes.

Everett set down his tool kit with a clatter and squatted beside it. He lifted out a rubber flashlight that he stuck in his mouth, pointing it with his head as both hands fiddled with valves and tubing.

"Want me to hold the light?" Steve asked.

Everett shook his head, streaking the beam from one stone wall to the other.

After ten minutes of manipulation, he wiped his hands across his coat and set down the flashlight. "You've got a mighty old furnace here. Low on efficiency. That's why you're not getting much heat on the second floor."

"What can you do?"

"Nothing much. Except replace it. With Martha managing the property, I wouldn't hold my breath."

"What about electric heaters?"

Everett snorted. "This wiring would go up like a torch."

When Steve told Debra, she threw a pot across the kitchen, gashing a cabinet. "Damn that woman! I hate her! Damn her to hell!"

In an instant of panic he pictured Julia, then realized she meant Martha Selig.

•

Steve got in his car and drove off toward town, desperate to talk to someone, intending to call Harold when he squeezed into the phone booth, but dialed Julia instead, trembling at the sound of ringing, afraid her husband would answer, realizing how much he missed their evenings together. He gulped when she answered, a sound like a sob. She agreed to meet him for a drink.

"It's like Martha Selig is responsible for everything that's wrong with her life," he said when they sat in a dim booth far from the TV set and the men at the bar who shouted at the ballplayers. "She's never even met the woman."

"Maybe it's easier to blame Martha," Julia said.

"Than who? Me?"

Julia shook her head. Steve realized that she had a new haircut, shorter, styled with a wave that accentuated her cheekbones. He wanted to tell her how good she looked. But when their eyes met, before he could say anything, she explained. "Than herself."

"For what? I'm the one who's supposed to provide. To make sure his kids don't freeze to death in their own house."

"Harold thinks Debra's the problem."

"Harold said that?"

Julia nodded. She reached across the table to touch his hand, and he seized hers in both his, not daring to look at her, sure she would pull away. But she didn't. They sat with their fingers intertwined.

Julia went on. "She's not the wife he would have picked for you."

Steve squeezed her hand, rubbed fingertips over the smooth knuckles, and stared at her with tear-blurred eyes. "Who would he have picked?"

"That never came up."

In the parking lot, he put an arm around her shoulder, the two of them leaning into the icy wind. At her car, he pulled her into him and bent to kiss her, but she turned the gesture into a hug and then brushed his face with her glove. He sat in his own car, watching the steam of her exhaust, the beams of her headlights, her car's slow movement across the snow-patched gravel, waiting long after she was gone before starting his own engine. Trembling, he touched his fingertips to his face and smelled the scent of her hair.

•

Harold appeared the next evening, stomping snow from his boots on the porch steps. Debra was in the kitchen staring at a water stain on the ceiling. When Steve let Harold in, she didn't come to the living room.

"I've got the perfect solution," Harold announced. "Move the kids downstairs where it's warm. Set up the cribs in the living room." He paused and smiled at Steve, as if expecting praise for his ingenuity.

But Steve only nodded. "Then it would be just like the apartment."

"Only for the winter. Hey, the year's full of months."

"How did you know about the heat problem?" Steve asked him.

"News travels."

Steve followed Harold outside and leaned over him as he sat in his car. "Why did you send Julia to me?"

"I thought she'd be good for you."

"In what way?"

"To give you perspective."

When Harold drove off, waving but facing straight ahead, Steve sensed it would be a long time before he saw him again.

●

Debra refused to help. She sat on a kitchen chair, tapping a pot against her toe. Steve put Timothy in Molly's crib so that he could disassemble his. The baby's sharp cries set off her much louder wailing. They wouldn't stop, one child echoing the other, the two of them so hysterical they quivered with breathless gasps.

Once Timothy's crib was set up in the living room, he moved both children downstairs and started on Molly's. The job took longer than he expected, bolting and unbolting, dragging frames and springs and mattresses down the narrow stairway.

"Come see," he told Debra when he finished. When she refused to move, he squeezed her wrists and tried to force her from the chair. She pushed him away and stared at the floor.

"I'm going out for beer," he announced. He slammed the door and tried to clear his windshield with the wipers, but the new snow was already too thick. He brushed it off with his bare hands, then had to suck his fingertips.

Before he went into the minimart, he called Julia. The phone rang a dozen times. Coming out, he tried again. This time a man answered, the voice rich and sure. "Wrong number," Steve muttered. He stood holding the phone, openmouthed, aching.

When he got back to the house, all the lights were out though it wasn't yet ten. In the living room, guided by moonlight, he saw the shapes of the babies swaddled in blankets. On the couch, surrounded by cribs, Debra huddled under all the comforters stripped from their bed, a dark lump. He watched the rise and fall of her breathing, suspecting she only pretended to sleep. Standing at the edge of the doorway, he turned from her to Molly and Timothy and back again. Shadows of crib bars fell across the bare floor. Still wearing his hat and jacket, Steve wrapped his arms around his chest and shuddered as if the chill would never leave him. He saw this woman and these children living in other rooms, in a home he would never know.

Visiting

Thomas hadn't seen his sister in three years, the last time six months before her marriage to Chuck. But when a business trip took him west to Kansas City, she insisted that he spend a long weekend with her and Chuck and the kids at their new home in Fort Shawnee.

"I bet you expected war whoops and hostile natives," Lynda said with a hug when he climbed out of the taxi. "Nothing but ordinary families around here these days." She gestured toward the sprawling green lawns and lush shrubs of a neighborhood much like the one in Oak Brook Park where she had lived when she was married to Peter and Chuck to Steffie. Thomas knew as soon as he saw it that he would always confuse the two houses, forever forgetting which had the red brick veneer and which the brown, which had the backboard on the side of the garage and which on the front.

"How's everything?" he asked.

"I'd almost forgotten I had a brother." Lynda braced arms on his shoulder, pulled back, and studied him from top to bottom. "You're the same old Tommy."

"Should I take that as a compliment?"

"My world's aswirl with changes. But brother Tom's my polar star."

"Don't you have a compass?"

"Me? I get lost walking from the frig to the patio."

She wore thigh-hugging shorts and a striped rugby shirt, in great shape for a woman of forty. Firm legs, square shoulders, a newly blonde streak in her short cropped hair. A few smile lines, otherwise a smooth tan face. "You're looking terrific," he told her, wondering how she had managed to stay so untouched.

"I work out religiously." She tried to pinch the flesh at her waist and came up empty handed.

•

Lynda led Thomas to a closed door in what she called the "sleeping wing." He followed, clutching his suitcase tight to keep it from knocking over the ceramic knickknacks in the hallway. "It's Debbie's. But she can use the rec room sofabed."

"Are you sure she won't mind?"

"Tough. How many times does Uncle Tommy come to visit?"

Debbie was Chuck's sixteen-year-old, who had seen Thomas twice in her life, both times when he was the brother of the lady next door. There were five kids all together — Lynda's boys, Adam in his late teens and Jonah in his early, and Chuck's Debbie, Nick, and Mark, the baby of the group at ten. It was mid-afternoon on a Friday and the kids were still in school, Chuck at work.

"Unpack yourself while I fix us a drink." Lynda disappeared around a corner.

Debbie's room smelled like a cosmetic counter from all the jars and creams and spray bottles lined across the vanity table. The bed was stripped, bright sheets folded atop the pillows, a matching spread heaped at the foot of the mattress, dragging on the rug. Glossy magazine photos of bare-chested rock stars hung crooked from pins in the delicate floral wallpaper.

Thomas unzipped his suitcase and flipped it open on the bed, emptying the compartments and squeezing his two suits onto a closet rod packed with designer jeans and silk blouses. He pulled out dresser drawers, assuming one had been emptied for him, and found the large ones stuffed with sweaters. Dozens of unopened pantyhose packets were stacked in the small top drawer on the left. In the one on the right a diaphragm lay atop a cushion of pink bikini panties.

•

Lynda wouldn't let him put the call to Grace on his charge card. "You're my guest! You're my brother!"

She dialed herself, tapping buttons on a stainless steel kitchen phone shaped like a wedge. "Grace? Hi! Guess who this is? We're holding your husband captive." A pause. "Oh, everything's wonderful here. And I know it's wonderful with you too. I could tell by one look at Tommy." Another pause. "You too, sweetie. Oodles of love to the kids." She handed the phone to Thomas.

"Tom?" Grace's voice was tentative. The sound of her comforted him. For years his job had required so many business trips that he was used to being away. But here in his sister's kitchen he missed his wife.

"Hi," he said. "I found them."

"Has she been drinking?" Grace was whispering, hissing the s's.

"No, no. Nothing like that." He found himself shaking his head to emphasize the denial.

"It must be bedlam with all those children."

"They're still in school. We're in a different time zone, remember?"

"Lynda's always been in another zone."

He nodded and returned the smile of his hovering sister.

"Kiss the girls for me," he said before he hung up. "Grace sends love," he told Lynda.

•

Thomas sat in Chuck's leather rec room recliner thumbing through the TV listings while Lynda mixed martinis in the kitchen. The side door slammed. "Leave me alone, you puss-faced turd!" "Shove it, you fat little wimp!" Two boys pushed their way into the room, the bigger one, his acned nephew Adam, elbowing the little one, who must have been Mark, so hard he tripped into the stereo rack. Mark kicked out and stung Adam's shin. Adam slapped him across the ear. "You bastard!"

"Hey!" Thomas called, but they didn't react to the sound.

When Adam hit him again, Mark howled, threw himself on the floor and yanked at fistfuls of shag carpet. Lynda walked in with a crystal pitcher and two stemmed glasses on a silver tray. "Where's

Jonah?" she asked Adam.

He shrugged. "Who gives a fuck?"

Mark slid across the carpet and tried to bite his ankle. Adam ground his other foot into Mark's buttock.

"Play outside boys," Lynda said, digging in a drawer for coasters. "I want to talk to your uncle."

"He's not my uncle," Mark cried. "I hate him!"

"It's not nice to hate people."

Mark punched Adam in the kidney and ran out onto the patio. Adam pounded up the steps to the top level, and twenty seconds later the house shook with the blast of his stereo.

"They pick on Adam and he picks back," Lynda told Thomas.

"Who's they?"

"All of them — Mark and Debbie and Nick. Even Jonah."

"Why?"

She went wide-eyed and blank, a gesture he remembered from the time she was five. "I've never understood children."

Jonah and Nick came in the back door, shouting lyrics of a punk song Thomas vaguely remembered seeing on a video, something about blood spurting from slashed wrists. They leaped from the kitchen to the rec room strumming imaginary guitars and gyrating pelvises.

"Hi," Jonah said and reached out to shake Thomas's hand. He was clearly Lynda's son, a goodlooking kid with a face that duplicated her straight nose and square jaw. Adam favored his father, a bond salesman with a penchant for order whom Lynda had accused of being rigid and obsessive through fifteen years of marriage.

Thomas pulled himself up from the lounger to meet his nephew's grip.

"Mom said you were coming. How's it going?"

"Fine. I'm glad to see you all again."

"This is Nick. He's my stepbrother now."

Nick shook hands too, a lanky boy with ringlets of red hair that started very low on his forehead and a goofy freckled face. But he was supposed to be very bright. "I think I met you once before in Oak Brook Park," Nick said.

"Very briefly, when you were much younger."

"Well, it's nice to see you again, sir."

"We have to practice now," Jonah said. "Catch you at dinner, Uncle Thomas."

"What are they practicing?" he asked Lynda when they left. "Their act, they say. But it's an excuse to go down into the basement and smoke grass."

"Don't you stop them?"

"It keeps them off the hard stuff. That's what Chuckie and I think." She poured herself another glass from the pitcher.

"They look healthy enough."

"Oh, it gives them the appetite of horses."

•

When Chuck signaled the automatic garage opener at six, Lynda had spread a dozen stainless steel bowls across the kitchen counter, chopping a cleaver against a wooden block, rattling spoons, whisking a wire beater. Thomas was watching the local news, a camera crew cornering the mayor with rapid-fire questions about a pothole crisis, a plump weatherman who kept wiggling his nose while the sportscaster cracked up in the background.

"Hey, old man!" Chuck stepped through the door from the garage to the rec room, beaming a smile, his aviators now replaced by contacts, hair thick at the temples to disguise his protruding ears. He's coifed, Thomas kept thinking while he stood and let the man hug him around the neck in a hearty embrace.

Lynda joined them from the kitchen, a lacy apron over a black cocktail dress, to stand beside Chuck, the two of them, arm in arm, stepping back from Thomas to beam at him.

"Hey, this is great," Chuck said, reaching out to shake hands again. "Say, how's Grace?"

"She's fine," he said.

"And the girls?"

"Fine too."

"That's sensational," Chuck said.

"Oh, I almost forgot my surprise," Lynda said. "Guess who's joining us for dinner?"

Thomas stood baffled. Aside from the people he had met at a business meeting yesterday, he knew no one within five hundred miles of this house.

"Steffie!" Lynda sang the name. "She's been shopping all day with my car."

"What Steffie?" He looked to Chuck to see if he had heard right. But Chuck was still gloating at the sight of him.

"You know what Steffie," Lynda said, waving a hand at him as if he were an absolute fool. "Chuck's ex. My best friend."

•

Seven of them were seated around the teak table, the chrome ceiling fixture set at a hazy low, three open wine bottles breathing on the sideboard behind them. Chuck had rearranged their places to put Thomas between Adam and Mark, so that Mark ended up in the captain's chair at the table's head making faces at Adam when he thought no one was looking. Adam just sulked. "Steffie should be here by now," Lynda said. "I told her seven-thirty and she repeated the time back to me. I can't imagine where she could be."

"Steffie's never on time," Chuck said. "You know that."

"And where's your sister?" Lynda asked Nick.

Nick looked at Jonah, and the two of them brought hands to their mouths to smother giggles. "With Dicky. Mr. Hunk." Jonah burst out laughing. Thomas pictured the naked diaphragm.

"The hell with them," Chuck said. "They'll just have to put up with cold bisque. Let's eat."

"Steffie will be so disappointed," Lynda said.

"I've got a hungry family," Chuck told her. "In another minute they'll be beating their silverware on the plates."

Which is what Mark started doing immediately.

"Shut up, asshole," Adam said.

"Chuckie, tell him that isn't nice," Lynda said.

Chuck poured wine for the adults and then filled Mark's glass. "I'm training his palate," he told Thomas.

The front door opened and a great hound dog came bounding into the dining room, hind end quivering as it whimpered with the joy of reunion. It pulled gums back and bared teeth in what looked like a grin, then nuzzled its snout into each lap at the table.

"That's Prince," Jonah told Thomas. "Steffie took him shopping."

"Prince loves Steffie," Lynda said.

"Prince Ferdinand of Ballantrae," Nick said.

"He's got papers," Jonah added. Thomas noticed how wide his pupils were, Nicks's too.

Prince licked Thomas's hand with a long, wet tongue.

Then Steffie entered the dining room with arms full of bright packages. She dropped them against the sideboard and swooped down to give Thomas a hug of welcome, a loud smooch on the cheek. "It's wonderful to see you again!"

They had met once in the driveway when he and Grace had visited Lynda and Peter seven years ago, exchanging pleasantries across the property line. Four years later when he stopped by alone on another business trip, she had just run off to Alaska with a Piper Cub pilot who was going to make a killing doing short hauls, abandoning her children, all her clothes, flying off on a whim, calling from Fairbanks to say goodbye. "And it wasn't because of me and Chuck," Lynda had assured Thomas then when she drove him to the airport. "Doesn't she care at all?" Thomas had asked her, and Lynda had responded as if explaining the obvious to a small child: "She knows we can't help loving each other."

Steffie was a tall, thin, long-waisted woman who seemed to slither when she moved. But her face was round and flat even with all the highlighting makeup, as if the wrong head had been superimposed on her body.

"You're just in time to eat," Lynda said.

"I bought the most wonderful things," she said, "and can't wait to show you."

Chuck had everyone pass plates to him and lifted the lid from the microwave dish. "Ummm. Doesn't that smell good?"

•

After a dessert of puffed pastry swimming in sticky caramel, the children vanished and Steffie called Prince to her room to watch her unwrap her packages. Thomas cleared the table despite Lynda's protests. "I want to help," he said.

He scraped leftovers into a garbage can, realizing how little Jonah and Nick had eaten, and then stacked plates on a kitchen counter. Lynda wouldn't let him load the dishwasher. "It can all wait. There's always the morning. Right, Chuckie?" Chuck nodded from a stool at the breakfast bar. The stove top was littered with crusted pans.

Lynda squeezed both Thomas's hands in hers and stepped back to get another good look at him. "I can't believe you're here. My big brother. Every day I say to Chuckie, all my life Tommy's been my polar star."

"Every day," Chuck echoed.

"I'm such a scatterbrain, but you've always had your head on straight. You've always known the right way to live. Whenever I have a problem, I think, what would Tommy do? When I knew I loved Chuck and he was married to my best friend, I said to myself, Tommy's the kind of person who always goes for the brass ring. So I went for it." She leaned over and smacked a kiss on Chuck's cheek, then one on Thomas's

I'm nothing like that, he thought.

•

At midnight, Mark asleep, Adam in his room with the throbbing stereo, Jonah and Nick in the basement again, Debbie still not home, the four adults sat in the rec room, Thomas and Chuck sharing a six-pack of Dinkelacker and Lynda and Steffie a pitcher of brandy alexanders. Chuck had tuned in to grand prix auto racing on ESPN with the sound down, cars circling around and around, some spinning out of control. Now and then Chucks's eyes would close, but he shook his head, blinked, and sat up straight in the lounger. "I'm not tired," he said each time he nodded. Prince sat at Thomas's feet, looking up soulfully, tapping his knee with a paw.

"I knew it was wrong with Peter and me from the start," Lynda was telling Steffie. "All my friends were getting engaged, all his. We just drifted into it from inertia. I was too young to know myself. I wanted so much to be in love." Thomas recalled how she had first spoken the exact words to him and Grace years ago, when Adam was a toddler. The story of her first marriage.

Steffie nodded, licking the foam from her glass before she poured another.

"I had doubts, but I forced them out of my head. There were so many wedding preparations I couldn't find time to think. We did nothing for a year but plan. Floral arrangements, gown alternations, menus, seating charts, color coordination. The wedding seemed like the purpose of my life. It was hard to believe there'd be a marriage afterwards. Was it like that with you and Chuck?"

"I don't remember."

"I cried at my wedding. Nobody saw me. When my mother and bridesmaids left the room, I broke down for five solid minutes, then had to put on my makeup all over again. But now I've got Chuck and I'm happy."

"It's so wonderful when people are happy," Steffie said.

She turned the pitcher upside down over her glass and slapped the bottom, eyes fixed on the slow trickle of the last drops.

•

Thomas excused himself slightly after one. "I've had a very long day." Chuck was snoring in the lounger, his face slack and grey, Lynda telling Steffie how Peter had always put her down for being sloppy. Steffie kept muttering, "I know, I know," now clutching a bottle of Remy Martin by the neck. When he left the room, Lynda blew him a kiss without a pause in her sentence.

67

An hour later, just as he was finally about to drift off in the strange room, the door opened and bright light flooded in from the hallway. Someone sat heavily at the foot of the bed. Thomas blinked himself back to consciousness, expecting Lynda with a need to chat or Debbie never told that she'd been displaced by a step uncle.

"Thomas." His name came out throaty and slurred. He focused and found Steffie.

"Is something the matter?" For a second his pulse raced with alarm.

She flopped full length beside him, her stale syrupy breath just inches away. "Let's get it on."

"What?"

"I can't sleep. I've got to do something."

"Play a record. Watch TV."

"What's the matter? Don't you like me?"

"I'm married."

"So's Chuck. We get it on every once in a while. For old time's sake. When he was married to me, he and Lynda got it on. Everybody's getting it on."

"Steffie, I'm faithful to my wife."

"Shit! You think you're some kind of superior being, don't you?"

"I'd just like to get some sleep."

He feared she would stay sprawled against him until he slid out from under the covers and took himself to a couch. But she pulled herself up and stumbled toward the doorway. "Fag! You couldn't get it up with a winch."

•

Slamming doors, shouting voices awakened Thomas. He lit his watch and saw that it was three-thirty in the morning. When he lifted his head from the pillow, he could make out words.

"You little tramp! Do you know what time it is?" That was Lynda.

"It's none of your business!" That must have been Debbie, high-pitched, arrogant.

"It's my house. You're living in my house!"

Lynda was the hysterical one. Debbie was just loud. "My dad pays the mortgage. You're the one sponging off my dad."

"How'd you like to be out on your cheap little ass?"

"He'd never do it. He hasn't got the guts."

"I'll do it! I'll kick you out myself!"

"You're not my mother."

"Your mother is my best friend."

"Then call her. Go ahead. Get her to wake up when she's pissed. Try it."

"You little bitch!"

Prince erupted into frantic barking.

•

At six in the morning Thomas came downstairs to brew himself coffee. After the racket in the middle of the night he wasn't able to sleep. And Prince had started scratching at his door, leaping up with paws on Thomas's chest when he finally opened it, then curling onto the foot of the bed.

Thomas expected the kitchen to be empty at that hour, but he found Lynda yawning at the table while the coffeemaker gurgled. Dinner dishes, toppled glasses, and dirty pans seemed to cover every surface. She squeezed his hand when he sat beside her. "It's so great having you here, Tommy. Just like when we were kids."

"We never did this when we were kids."

"You know what I mean."

He didn't.

Lynda poured the coffee and took a box of frozen donuts from the freezer. "Hungry?"

"I can't eat sweet things so early."

"It's all I can."

He watched her for a minute and finally brought himself to speak. "What's between you and Debbie?"

She shrugged. "I let her get to me. She's going through a rebellious thing."

"Can't Chuck talk to her?"

"Chuck? She plays daddy's little girl and he melts."

"Steffie then. She's her mother."

"Steffie's still traumatized about the thing with Lance."

"The pilot?"

"You mean Wayne. That was years ago. After Wayne there was Shawn and then Lance."

"What about Adam and Mark? Are they always like that?"

"It's just a phase. Adam's having hormonal changes."

"What about Jonah and Nick?"

"They're the good ones. They never bother me."

"But they're stoned most of the time."

"All the ninth graders are like that."

"Are you sure it's right for all of you having Steffie around?"

"Why on earth would you say that? I can confide in Steffie. We're closer than sisters."

"Isn't there anything you want to tell me now?" Thomas asked.

"About what?"

"Your life."

She blinked up at him, eyes dazzled with bewilderment.

Pleasure

They flew down the snow-packed hill on aluminum disks, plastic sheets, tiny children's sleds, crashing into drifts, each other, rolling over and over until they lay spreadeagled at the base of the trees, the cluster of Sally's friends Michael had just met that afternoon, one more stoned than the next, screaming into the wind. Michael couldn't remember any of their names or who was supposed to be with whom. The bloated babyfaced man in orange earmuffs was Leroy or Leslie, his wife one of two scrawny little women, either the one jabbering some incessant anecdote about her cat or the one whining about having to go to the toilet. Harry or Henry, who stood heaving snowballs at the others, was supposed to be hopelessly in love with Emma or Edna, a selfish bitch, now off flirting with somebody named Don or Tom, whose wife had stayed home in protest. Sally had talked of these people for hours, the tangles of their relationships, the traumas of their lives. Finally meeting them, Michael could not associate their faces with the tales of alcoholism, adulteries, breakdowns, and attempted suicides. They all looked so ordinary. He watched Sally rush from one to the other — hugging, squeezing gloved hands, kissing cheeks. Then he shrugged and flopped into a snowpile, lying motionless in the powdered chill until Ed or Ted or Fred pulled him out.

•

He liked to call Sally, listen to her say, "Hello, Michael," as if really pleased that it was him. Her voice was soft and sensual, warm with a throaty pleasure. More than anything else he enjoyed hearing her on the phone, when his imagination could make her into anyone he wished. Some nights he would sit in darkness and dial her number again and again just for the sound of her greeting.

•

On a whim, Michael decided to introduce Sally to Gene, a courtly Southerner he had known for years but usually avoided. They sat around a table littered with lobster shells and wine bottles, Michael snapping at Sally's nose with a hollow claw while Gene sprawled back in his chair and stretched out his long legs. "I did it with a woman once," Sally was telling Gene, who had introduced the question of sex. "I wanted to find out whether I'd like it." "Did you?" Gene asked. "No. It was weird. Women aren't the answer for me." "Is Michael?" Sally just smiled, but Michael laughed so hard that even the waiters stared.

•

With his wife Michael had never done anything. "Sat home and watched the kids grow" was what he told people after they separated, remembering how one night he went out into the yard and howled his boredom at the moon. He would demonstrate the sound for strangers, again and again, until Sally clamped a hand over his mouth and pinched his nostrils shut.

•

Sally threw a party for herself because her birthday came a week before Christmas and never received enough attention. Michael set up the bar while she warmed the hors d'oeuvres. Within a half hour the apartment was jammed with people, most new to him. Lois and Carl were there, Harvey too. Someone named Leonard came wearing lipstick, and that upset Tim, who spent the whole evening in handclenched agitation. Ruth danced on the coffee table and stepped high heels into the avocado dip. Joe and Elizabeth had an argument, and she insisted on telling everyone about his premature ejaculations. Ralph and Vera made out behind the drapes, while Ralph's wife, Terry, tried to paw at Will, who was more interested in setting up Sally's bong. Lenore crashed into the tension pole shelves and scattered knickknacks. People kept turning up the stereo, and the neighbor below pounded on the ceiling. Someone reported that Lou had passed out in the parking lot, his cheek frozen to a hubcap. Charlie and Vic went to look. Sally tripped on her way from the kitchen to the living room and dumped a pan of steaming lasagna onto the shag carpet. When everyone was gone, she told Michael it was the best party she had been to all year.

•

Before driving out into the winter night they had spent half an hour sucking smoke from the syrupy residue in Sally's hash pipe. Now they couldn't find their way to a party at a place they had never been before. Headlights, traffic signals, neon signs all fragmented and multiplied in Michael's vision. Blazes of green, blue, yellow, red. At an intersection, dazzled, he swerved into a sudden left turn. For an instant another car faced them head on, then veered with a shriek of tires. Michael slammed brakes and spun a circle on the icy shoulder, spraying gravel against the undercarriage. Sally sat beside him in rigid silence, but he blared the horn because they had come within a hair of being killed.

•

Her back to him, just beyond the reach of his fingertips, Sally kicked out of her jeans, pulled off her tee shirt, and dropped a gown over her head. From the pillows Michael saw her through smokestung eyes, a grey shape in the first glow of dawn. The mattress sagged them

73

together as she climbed under the covers. When their legs tangled, he touched her arm and she slid against him. Her warm flesh softened, but he would not tighten his grip, would not close his eyes. She rolled away and within moments sprawled in openmouthed sleep, while Michael lay awake listening to the soft whistle of her breathing and staring out at the litter of objects that emerged from the darkness — a sweater balled on the dresser, a brassiere dangling from a lamp, letters stuck into the mirror frame. He wondered whom she wrote to, who wrote to her, what she had to say to anyone.

Clogged

Things kept going wrong. This time her rec room toilet overflowed. She flushed and watched helplessly as the water just sat shimmering for several seconds and then rose with the emptying of the tank until it spilled over the edge of the bowl onto the bathroom tiles. Next the pipes backed up, churning out a sludge of toilet paper, hair, and feces. Oh, how it stank! And it wouldn't stop, a stream of sewage flowing from the bathroom onto the kitchen linoleum, seeping into the rec room rug.

Cynthia screamed, a futile high-pitched shriek, until she thought to call her son's name: "Tommy! Tommy! Tommy!" The boy came thumping down from the second floor in tee shirt, boxer shorts, and unlaced hunting boots, calling back "Mom! Mom! Mom!" He moved with an adolescent gawkiness, his large boned frame not yet filled out with his father's bulk.

He looked at the mess and stopped short. "Oh, Jesus!"

"Do something!" Cynthia cried, tears of frustration burning down her face. "Do something. I just can't cope anymore."

It had been a terrible week, one disaster after another. She had a habit of tabulating them in her mind, running through the list several times a day to see if there was something she had missed, another item to add to the total, as if unwillingly setting some sort of record: never had a woman more woe than she. Yet, if you asked her, as people often did in one way or another, she would have insisted that she sought only a life of joy.

But here was this week's list: a rusted out muffler on the Ford, no rinse cycle on the washer, an ingrown toenail, a blown picture tube, Tommy's new down jacket ripped on barbed wire, Ginny's only pair of school shoes worn through, an overdue warning from the gas company, two bounced checks, menstrual cramps.

And those were only things. The people in her life were driving her crazy too. Not people — men. Unless you counted her ex-mother-in-law, who was always whining about not having seen the children in six months, and her neighbor Barbara, who was a perpetual bitch. But the men — they were impossible. Charlie, her supervisor, had turned in a bad evaluation, complimentary on the surface, but devastating between the lines. George, her ex-husband, missed his child support payment again, called to beg forgiveness, and ended up abusing her drunkenly. Bob, her one-time lover, now "doing good" with a muffler franchise in Tucson, wrote a long letter of graphic reminiscence in which he promised a surprise visit "someday soon." Herb, her lecherous neighbor, propositioned her at the back fence again. And twice she couldn't keep from calling Neal at one in the morning to make him tell her all the things he would do if he were in her bed. Then she lay awake with remorse. She didn't want to long so much for any man. She just wanted to be left alone, to have a simple uncomplicated life, to be in control.

Ginny edged down the stairs in a nightgown and puffy pink slippers, stood on the bottom step, and groaned, "Yuk!" while Tommy splashed through the mess to turn off the water valve. The flooding stopped, but the kitchen and half the rec room were covered with sewage.

"Now what do we do?" Cynthia looked at her house and wanted to run, hop into the Ford to drive fast and far. Except that the car might not start, and even if it did, she would probably asphyxiate on carbon monoxide.

"Call a plumber," Tommy said.

"Plumber? I can't afford a plumber. I can't afford a muffler and a coat and shoes. I can barely afford for us to eat. Can't you fix it?"

"I'm just a kid."

"You're fifteen years old and six feet two. The least you could do is unstuff a drain."

"How about Dad?"

"What about him?"

"He's great at fixing things. I bet he'd come right over if I called him."

"Forget your father." As soon as she said it, Cynthia regretted her tone. She wasn't up to justifying her divorce to her son again.

"Tommy wants you and Dad to get together," Ginny said. "Remarry like those people on TV did. I think it'd be neat too."

"This is not time to talk about your father. My house is buried in —" Cynthia stopped herself at the last second.

"Shit," Tommy said. Ginny giggled.

"Don't use words like that. Do something."

"I'll call Mr. Wittner."

"No, no, no," Cynthia insisted. Mr. Wittner was the lecherous Herb, the man who an hour after George loaded his car and slammed the door to drive away forever had approached her to offer his services "any time you've got the urge for a man." No, she definitely did not want to seek out the neighborly Mr. Wittner for help. "Let's not bother him if we don't have to."

"We have to," Tommy said. "Mr. Wittner, Dad, or a plumber."

At least he didn't include Neal on his list. Of course, he had no reason to. Neal had only been to the house a few times, at least while Tommy and Ginny had been awake, once to help her with taxes, another time to mat a new print. As far as Cynthia's children knew, he was just another acquaintance, not the man who made her quiver on the rec room rug.

"Here's what we'll do," she said. "You and I will try to fix it ourselves first. If we can't, we ask Mr. Wittner. Ginny, you go to sleep."

"I can't. It smells like a sewer."

"Open your window."

"It'll always smell awful." Ginny began to weep. Cynthia moved to comfort her and then realized the stuff was all over her shoes. She would track it through the house if she went to her daughter.

First, Tommy tried a plunger, splashing over more gunk when he pushed into the bowl. He pumped and pumped, but could not break the jam.

Cynthia leaned against the sink and watched him. His face seemed about to collapse, the way it did when he was five and a toy broke, when he would burst into tears and wrapped his arms about his father's knees. "Can I do anything?" she offered.

"Get a hanger and untwist it. Maybe I can jab the junk loose."

"What do you think it is?"

"In this house it could be anything. Probably Ginny's Tampax. That kid doesn't know anything about having periods."

"Oh, my God!"

"What?" He stopped to stare at his mother.

"Nothing." Panic burned at her cheeks. Neal had flushed a condom down that toilet. What if it should come floating back into the room? Flop beside Tommy's shoe? She wished she could make him stop, just leave everything.

When Cynthia straightened a coat hanger from the hall closet, Tommy poked down into the drain pipe. "I feel something. But I can't get at the right angle. I'll have to disconnect the bowl."

The boy unbolted the toilet from the floor, loosening the fitting with the big wrench his father had left in the garage. Despite everything, Cynthia enjoyed watching her son work, felt pride in his mechanical skill. But even with the toilet out of the way he couldn't clear the drain, just poked furiously with the hanger in an eruption of temper. "Bitch! Bastard!" This time she let him swear.

"I'm going to call Mr. Wittner," he told her.

"Do you have to?"

"What else can I do?"

"I don't know."

Before Tommy could pick up the wall phone, someone tapped on the back door and the boy opened it to Herb Wittner in rubber boots with a tool chest, power drill, and plumber's snake. He winked at Cynthia but spoke to Tommy. "Figured you'd be needing me. I was up in the attic and happened to look out the window. Saw the mess on your kitchen floor and the plunger leaning against the wall."

He was peeping again! Cynthia wanted to scoop up a handful of the slop and fling it in his face. The horny pervert still watched her! One day at the back fence he had told her how he waited up nights just to follow the pattern of lights on and off behind the shades when she went to bed: kitchen, bathroom, bedroom. "Leave me alone!" she had cried. "I want you so bad I ache," he had whined.

Herb Wittner was a fool. Every woman in the neighborhood said so. He tried to act like a stud, running fingers through his hair for a tousled look. But the rest of him was ridiculous — the thick bifocals, the beer belly ballooning out over his bandy legs, the duck waddle of his walk. Tommy liked him though, as did most of the teenaged boys on the block, because he took them and his sons out to a target range with an arsenal of collectors' rifles. He could field strip a carbine in twenty seconds, rebuild a carburetor in twenty minutes, feats guaranteed to impress adolescents.

He was also good at plumbing, sloshing right through the sewage and organizing Tommy to get to work on the drain. He clamped the snake to the drill bit, gave it torque to cut into the blocking sludge.

Amid the drill buzz and metal clatter, the phone rang. When Cynthia glanced at the kitchen clock and saw it was past midnight, she knew exactly who it was and, knees near buckling, kicked off her shoes in the hallway and hurried up to the bedroom extension.

Neal insisted on coming to help, and she wanted him so badly just hearing him on the phone that she had to press her fist between her thighs. But she made herself tell him not to come over. Tommy would think his being there strange. And what about Herb? The two of then in the same room? No, she couldn't. Neal declared urgent love, but she didn't dare whisper back, afraid someone might overhear. He finally hung up, and she had to clutch the bedspread to catch her breath.

When Cynthia returned downstairs, the drain was clear, Tommy telling Mr. Wittner how great he was. By the time the man and boy replaced the toilet, smeared pipe dope, and fastened all the fittings, it was two a.m., Tommy stumbling half asleep, more burden than aid. Herb told him to go to bed. "I have to help Mom clean up," the boy said.

"Forget it. I'll help your mother."

Cynthia couldn't protest. Her son was exhausted.

Somehow Herb knew where she kept her mops and plastic bucket. She followed his instructions silently, hesitant to flush down the bucket after bucket he mopped up even though he said it would be all right.

When they were clean, she poured straight Lysol onto the floors and started to drag the rec room rug out to the back yard.

"Needs a good cleaning anyway," Herb said.

She went rigid. "What do you mean?"

"Nothing." He smirked. "Just that a rug like that gets a lot of traffic."

He pulled it from her hands and yanked it out the back door, heaped it on the patio. Then he told Cynthia he had to run home for a piece of equipment. After ten minutes she gave up on him, assumed he had decided to go to sleep, was ready to go upstairs herself, when — on an impulse — she dialed Neal.

But at the first ring the door closed hard and she turned to find Herb in clean clothes and shower-wet hair, fixing her with a leering grin. She hung up quickly, grabbing a sponge and moving into the bathroom. He followed at once.

"I'm here all the time," he said. "Just across the fence. All you'd have to do is flash your lights and I'd come running."

"I don't want to hear it." She turned her back to him.

He pushed her against the sink, clutched one arm around her waist and reached the other hand over her shoulder, fingertips on her breast. Cynthia could see it all in the medicine cabinet mirror, the man half swooning, his glasses dangling off one ear.

She looked closely at her reflected face, the loosening of her jaw, the lines around her eyes. "I'm not that pretty," she said calmly, as if she were alone.

Herb pressed a wet mouth to her throat and emitted gasping groans. She wondered if Neal would look as foolish to a stranger and watched tears running down her face.

A sound startled her, the slightest creak of wood, and Cynthia turned to see her son on the stairway in his pajamas. She didn't know, couldn't guess, how long he had been standing there.

"I wanted to make sure everything was fixed," the boy blurted and ran up the steps.

She stood frozen for a second, then went after him, reached the second floor just as his bedroom door slammed. When he did not respond to her knock, she entered the room and crossed into the shaft of moonlight. Tommy's face was lost in darkness. She spoke his name, but he lay absolutely still. She listened carefully for his breathing and heard rapid swallows.

"Tommy, I want you to listen to me. It was him. He's a sick unhappy man. I've never done anything like that. You have to believe me." Cynthia waited, tempted to turn on a light so she could see his eyes, appeal to her son's gentle eyes. "Do you?" she pleaded.

The boy gulped. "Yes."

She dropped to her knees at his bedside and embraced him with tears.

When she went back downstairs, Herb was gone. He had taken his tool chest but left his snake on the bathroom tiles. Cynthia lifted it with two fingertips, carried it to the door, and tossed it as hard as she could toward the back fence. Then she began spraying the house with room deodorizer, pressing the hissing valve until she gagged on the chemical sweetness.

Petrushka

The second time Stefan made love to her, he played Stravinsky's Petrushka at a volume so intense she cried out, "The neighbors! The neighbors!" — her cries soaring with the pulse of the music.

The first time he made love to her, she — who had once believed first love was forever — huddled against a wall and whimpered shame, weeping while he stroked her face and murmured his devotion. At home again after she left Stefan, after clinging to him in his doorway, she had cried for hours as the children passed back and forth outside the bedroom and Dave grilled hamburgers on the patio. Her stomach churned at the fumes of charred beef. "What's wrong?" Dave had demanded, but she could only shake her head at her husband and grieve. After he and the children ate, he gave her an aspirin and drove off in her car. By the time, long after midnight, he came home drunk and fell upon her, she was dry-eyed, calm with the certainty that she would go back to Stefan again and again.

Dave, oversized, swollen with muscles, had mocked Stefan from the first time she invited him home for dinner, soon after he was transferred to her office, long before she knew she loved him. Stefan was frail and small, an educated man who cherished books and music, music always, in the house and car, even in his office, tuned low so that no one could complain. "I need music to think," Stefan had told her, "to live."

After the second time, whenever she returned to Stefan, *Petrushka* was already playing, programmed to repeat continuously, soft in the background while they shared wine and touched hands. But when the touching became urgent, the volume would rise with the surging horns, the staccato swirls of the strings. Finally, when their intimacy was complete, she asked him why this one piece, why *Petrushka*. "It's the most perfect music I know," he told her. "It brims with life. Even tragedy is only a moment in the festival." "What tragedy?" she asked. "Death — but of a puppet, just sawdust inside."

He gave her a taped copy, a surprise pressed into her hand like a treasure, the title of the movements written on a card in his precise script, shapes that she knew were a secret love note. She couldn't bring herself to play it, even when she was alone in her car, afraid of losing control. She would reach in her purse for the plastic case and snatch her hand away as if she had touched a dangerous object.

At home, all the hours away from Stefan, she moved as if she had forgotten something of great importance, suddenly seizing one of the children in a desperate embrace. When he was with them, Dave stumbled from room to room, flailing arms in anger, and she couldn't make herself speak to him, just watched his movements like a spectator. When she tried to explain to Stefan, he said. "You're drunk from love and he from alcohol."

Then in the middle of the night, awakened by poundings from the living room, she stepped out into the hallway to find the lamps glaring and Dave smashing her purse against a wall, gouging long dark streaks into the plaster. "Where do you go?" he demanded.

"I'm here most of the time," she insisted. "It's you who is always out."

"I know where I go. Not what you do."

"I have friends, people I like to talk with."

"Stefan, Stefan, Stefan." He squealed the name in a falsetto. "Goddamn music. That's all he's good for. To talk about goddamn music." He opened her purse upside down and dumped it on the carpet, immediately reaching for the tape case. "His goddamn faggot music."

She rushed against him, leaping up for the plastic box he held high above her head. She could see the children's door open, eyes peering out from the darkness. She beat at his chest, kicked at his toes, and Dave lisped, "Oh, music is so beautiful."

When she bit the flesh above his collarbone, he cried out and slapped her face so hard she fell over the coffee table. He reeled back into a chair and moaned at his pain. But he had dropped the tape case; it lay in the middle of the carpet, the two halves split apart.

She scrambled toward the stereo and forced the cassette into the deck, not daring to breathe for the seconds of silence before the first flute notes sang through the room. "It's the sound of you," Stefan had told her, "waking me to life." Sharp string chords responded. She saw Dave clutch his shoulder, then stare in disbelief at the smear of blood on his palm. He said something to her, and she twisted up the volume knob. He shouted and she turned the music still louder, surges of brass, a mournful waltz, he ranting and she refusing to hear, forcing the knob all the way. By the time he rose and stumbled toward her, the house was swollen with a noise that was no longer *Petrushka*.

Gone

Although it never occurred to him that she could ever disappear, Dale knew Gretchen was gone the moment he walked into the kitchen and saw the perfect order of the room: the sink empty of dishes, counter tops gleaming, chairs aligned under the table, the mildewed books that were usually strewn across every surface piled neatly on a cabinet.

He had entered that kitchen expecting to smell dinner in the oven, see Gretchen stooped over the stove in a twisted apron, stirring a pot with one hand, holding a book in the other, its pages splattered with a brown sauce, spots on her glasses; she would glance up distracted at the sound of him, as if she had to recollect his existence every time she saw him.

Dale understood immediately that she had worked for hours to obliterate every sign of her life in that room, like a thief wiping fingerprints.

A scrap of paper on the linoleum was the only object out of place; it must have slipped from one of the books. She was always writing down thoughts and then abandoning them between pages. He stooped to pick it up and stared at the two words scrawled in pencil as if they were very important, as if he would not be able to begin thinking what to do next until he deciphered them. " Hurry," they might have said, " hurry, hurry."

He imagined holding the paper out and asking what she had meant, and she blinking back the panic in those myopic grey eyes.

Dale folded the paper carefully, put it in his wallet, and moved out to the hallway. Her shapeless grey coat was missing from the rack. He stood at the foot of the stairs squeezing his hands open and shut, unable to make himself take the first step. But he could imagine what he would find, as vividly as if he were actually there: her dresser drawers vacant, a row of barren hangers dangling in her half of the closet.

And the children's room. Joseph's bed empty, Daniel's crib. The windows thrown open, curtains flapping in the wind, as if fairies had spirited them away. He shuddered with the certainty that he would never see his children again.

Then he heard a whimper, Daniel rolling over in a wet diaper, and he bolted up to them. Both boys were fast asleep, Joseph hugging a toy rabbit, Daniel hunched on his stomach in a yellow sleep suit. He had kicked his blanket off again. Dale reached through the crib bars to spread it over him, touching his hair, rubbing the fine strands between his fingers.

Why were they here? Gretchen was obsessed by her children. She always fixed them with her eyes as if expecting something to go terribly wrong. Dale was more stunned by the realization that she had abandoned her children than by her leaving.

When he realized how hungry he was, he went back down to the kitchen and took two pieces of bread from the loaf. He sat at the table to eat them, biting deep into an empty sandwich and chewing a doughy wad.

Through the night he had to climb up the stairs a dozen times to convince himself the children still existed. He kept expecting Gretchen to rush in the door, say, " How could I have forgotten?" and run back out with a boy under each arm.

•

Dawn took him by surprise. He couldn't recall the last time he had been awake at such an early hour. The kitchen suddenly glowed with brightness. The night was over, and he knew that she would never come back, that her leaving had been inevitable since the day they first spoke on the street, as if she had meant to turn away from him after his greeting and just remembered to complete the action.

Dale felt a great need for coffee. He opened cabinet doors until he found the can and then had to hunt another five minutes for the filters. He knew so little about this kitchen, even how much coffee to measure into the electric pot. Gretchen always took care of such things. In the mornings when he finally shook off the grey weight of sleep, a coffee aroma filled the house, and he would find her reading at the stove as if she had never slept.

Daniel broke the silence with a loud wailing and, immediately, Joseph began calling, " Mommy, Mommy." It struck Dale that he would have to change the baby's diaper, explain Gretchen's absence for his older son, and feed and dress them both. Then he would tell his company he would not be in that day while he found someone to care for his children.

From evening to morning his life had undergone a convulsion. But Dale would not admit to himself how lost he was. He would face one task at a time: change the diaper, feed his sons, dress them, call work, arrange day care, and then — if there was still time — search for Gretchen.

•

It took all day to locate a woman who would watch the boys. He would bring them to her house two towns away and then double back to his company. The woman, a Mrs. Kulka, was a plump, grey-haired grandmother who watched five other children, infants and toddlers, in a paneled basement. Although she smiled all though their conversation, Dale didn't believe she really liked children. She studied his sons huddled against his chair, away from the play of the others, as if they were unknown animals who might turn vicious. Mrs. Kulka made Dale sign an agreement and asked for five hundred dollars in advance.

The hunt for the sitter made him realize how isolated he and Gretchen had been. There was no one in the community he could call for advice, no friend to trust with his dilemma. They had lived their days in each other, apart from others, not even playmates for the boys. " I'm no good with people," Gretchen was always saying; but he knew she preferred seclusion, reading through the day, a book pulled up close to her eyes, passing hours without her revealing her face.

Her books were ancient, salvaged from forgotten trunks, bound with knotted cord in someone's basement. Yellowed page corners were always flaking off, littering the rugs wherever she walked. The books were trivial, all on obsolete subjects, written by authors long forgotten. But Gretchen took them so seriously that Dale never had the heart to comment.

She urged him to read her favorites, keeping him awake long into the night for earnest discussions, so that it was often an effort for him to get up in the morning. Even when he wanted so much to sleep, when the turns of her logic bewildered him, he never stopped being amazed that he was actually listening to a woman who was his wife, that children who called him Daddy slept on the other side of that wall.

•

Dale put the boys to bed, Joseph chanting " Where's Mommy? Where's Mommy" through his bath, louder and louder when Dale could think of no answer to give. He sat in the living room, not turning on a lamp, preferring the darkness.

Just a day had passed since he discovered Gretchen was gone, exactly twenty-four hours; but it seemed like years, as if their marriage were a memory from the life of a distant relation.

He told himself there hadn't been time to begin his search, yet knew that was a deception. In truth, he hadn't known where to start, where in the world she might have gone. He couldn't imagine Gretchen any place outside their house. She wouldn't drive, had refused to learn. They were miles from a train station or a bus line. Dale was sure she hadn't gone back to her parents. Her marriage to him had enraged them. There was no contact; she never spoke of them. In her whole life she knew only two places: the town where they had grown up and the town where they lived now. She had no friends. He was the only human being she had ever been close to.

Dale wished there were someone he could confide in. Although he kept a photo of Gretchen and the children on his desk, no co-worker ever commented. Their conversations had never gotten beyond company gossip. The news would only upset his parents, not that they cared for Gretchen. Her flight would confirm their suspicions. "Why are you marrying that girl?" his mother had said, shocked at his announcement. Yet a missing daughter-in-law would be a terrible embarrassment. He was ashamed to tell his older brothers even though they were thousands of miles away, both successful men, smug in their happiness.

Dale pulled his feet up onto the chair, hugged his knees to his chest, and cried, so softly a person sitting across the room would have been unsure what the sound meant.

•

They met the summer he graduated from college. That was the way he always thought of their coming together, though meeting was an odd term to describe the changed relationship of two people who had shared twelve years in the same classrooms.

Planning to go on to divinity school, Dale worked tending the grounds of the Methodist Church, as he had every summer since the ninth grade. Reverend Coolidge would spend hours with the boy, keeping him from his work, rehearsing subjects for his sermons, selecting books from his shelves that Dale should read. From the time he was thirteen, Dale had spent thousands of hours discussing books someone else had chosen for him.

All his life he had been known as a serious boy. His older brothers had been athletic and social. Only they were disappointed in him. Everyone else seemed to accept him for what he was — studious, well-mannered, dull. His classmates sought his advice on homework but had little else to say to him.

It was Gretchen they mocked for her grades, though he was the one the teachers turned to for answers, while she sat in the back row looking ridiculous as she tried to shrink her long thick body into invisibility. Her knees jutted out from under the desk. Her hair hung tangled to her shoulders. Her eyes blurred behind thick glasses. But for all her odd features, the others probably would have teased much less if she had different parents, not the couple who spent seven days a week in their tiny grocery store, overcharging for dust-covered canned goods, shouting abuse at each other in an endless quarrel even in the presence of customers. The mother was a buxom woman, tightly corseted, always formal in dark dresses. The father was a sunken man with a sullen face who pounded the keys of the cash register as if furious at the machine.

The majority found Gretchen laughable. A few pitied her. Dale had always envied her intelligence, certain it reached genuine insights, while his was the result of calculated effort.

That summer he began noticing her passing each day on the sidewalk in front of the church, stoop-shouldered, eyes fixed on the pavement, moving with a stiff-kneed lunge, as if she had learned how to walk from a book with incomplete instructions.

The first few times Dale saw her he was up on a ladder washing the stained glass windows. He wanted to call down a greeting but feared startling her. Then he planned to be trimming hedges at the time she usually came by. The first few days he pretended he didn't see her but finally made himself step onto the sidewalk and say hello.

She paused abruptly, blinked at him as if trying to remember why he was familiar, and then said, "I heard you finished college." It was the first time she had ever spoken to him.

"Yes, last month."

"It must have been a very rewarding experience."

"I enjoyed it very much."

"It's so wonderful. To be able to learn."

"You could have gotten scholarships." As soon as Dale said it he regretted the words, hoping she would not suspect a deliberate cruelty.

"Oh, I won several scholarships. My parents wouldn't allow me to go," she said.

"For God's sake, why not?"

"They say I'm all they have in the world." A thin smile passed across her face. "They couldn't bear to be without me."

"Do they make you work for them?" He saw her imprisoned in that narrow little store.

"I help. But they don't really need me. I have hours for reading. There are so many books and so much I don't know about the world."

No one had ever said such a thing to Dale. But he sensed that his questions had merely given her an excuse to speak aloud, that if he did not ask another immediately she would move on and forget they ever had this conversation.

"Would you like to meet me some time?" he blurted.

"Meet? We're meeting now."

"When there's really time to talk."

She looked at him as if he had made a remarkable suggestion. "All right," she finally said.

Two weeks later he told her he loved her, that he wanted to find a real job and marry her.

"You're going to be a reverend."

"I don't need that now. I have you."

"I never expected to be married," she said as if referring to a distant past.

"And I never thought that I would be able to ask someone."

"What if I don't know how to be a wife?"

He laughed and, for the first time, kissed her. It felt so wonderful to embrace her and bury his hands in the thick twists of her hair.

•

Dale had expected the boys to stop asking, as if Gretchen would vanish from their memories. But it became a daily ritual, Joseph's first words each morning, echoed by Daniel's inarticulate syllables: "Where's Mommy?" And he would answer, "Away." "When will she come back?" "When it's time."

That seemed to pacify Joseph, or at least silence him. Dale took the exchange to be an end in itself, a ceremony of lost meaning. But one evening, after his bath, the boy surprised him: "Does Mommy love us?" "Of course she does." "Then why isn't she here?" "She has to be somewhere else."

Her mistake had been answering him on the street that day, and his had been attempting to fight his true nature. He had been meant to live alone. He had known from the beginning that he would fail in his dream of normality.

•

Months passed before Dale could tell his parents. During their calls they spoke of his sons and his work. They never asked about Gretchen, not once during their marriage. And she never said a word to them, refusing to answer the phone: "No one ever calls me." Then he made himself say it, phoning with the intention of doing it at once, but waiting through ten minutes of hesitant conversation before he could blurt, "Gretchen's gone. She left me."

"When?" his mother asked, abrupt, angry.

"It's been a while. A long while."

"But the boys are with you. You tell us about them."

"Yes. They're fine."

Her questions were all of concern for her grandchildren. His explanation of the arrangement with Mrs. Kulka pacified her. "They must be happy," she insisted. "Promise me that you'll never let them suffer."

"I will," he told her but had no idea how to bring happiness to another human being.

His brothers called the next evening, first Clark and then Glenn, although the conversations were identical. He hadn't spoken to either of them in a year, and their voices seemed strange to hear. Mainly he listened, hoping Daniel would cry and give him an excuse to hang up.

Why hadn't he looked for his wife? they both wanted to know. Why hadn't he called the police? He assumed the police wouldn't help; there was no crime; she had chosen to leave. Both brothers offered to hire detectives, insisted on it. "No, no," Dale repeated, shaking his head with denial.

He knew his brothers cared nothing for Gretchen or even for his marriage. They had always been embarrassed that he had such a wife. Now they were even more ashamed that she had fled from him, furious with Dale for not being like them.

To pacify them he advertised in newspapers across the country, a note in the personal column: "Please come back to us. Dale, Joseph, Daniel." He couldn't imagine her looking at those pages. She never read newspapers, had no interest in public events. No woman on earth was harder to reach than Gretchen. He could spend decades living in a room next door and not know she was there.

•

The days were so much alike that Dale felt frozen in an endless present, each new year a meaningless number. He worked, tended to the boys in the evening, cleaned and laundered while they slept, prepared the next day's meals. Eventually Joseph started school and three years later Daniel. Mrs. Kulka faded from their lives. The boys made friends; they were so well-behaved, mothers reported and sought their visits in the after-school hours.

Dale sensed that they needed him less and less. Their exchanges were functional: what food would they like for the week, did they need new shoes, had they done their homework. Others amused them with trips to parks and movies and ice cream stores. Before they left the house, they would stand silently while he combed careful parts into their thick hair, his hand trembling as he held himself ready for screams that never came.

•

When Gretchen was gone for seven years, his brothers began a campaign of calls to make him file for divorce on grounds of desertion. "What difference would it make?" he told them. "We're apart now. We'll be apart forever."

It's messy, they argued. You have to put your life in order. Get rid of loose ends.

Dale called the local bar association for the names of divorce lawyers. The first on the list was a woman, a Melissa Eldridge. He scheduled the appointment for his lunch hour so that he would not have to make explanations to his co-workers.

Ms. Eldridge had a small office that opened directly onto a corridor. He had expected a reception room and a secretary, and was startled to pull back the door and walk in on a woman with brittle blonde hair talking into a recording machine. She looked quickly at her watch, blushed, and stood to shake his hand.

She was as tall as Gretchen; that was his first thought about her. But she was very thin and angular, with a large beaked nose too big for her face. Dale was sure her hair was dyed, surprised that he had noticed such a thing.

She let him speak, took notes, and then said, "You're my first desertion case."

"Is it that rare?"

"No, it's just that I'm new at all this." She laughed and blushed again. "I guess that's not the sort of thing you're supposed to tell clients. Not every reassuring."

Her awkwardness calmed him. He was nervous too, sure that this first step on the way to divorce would disrupt the bland calm of his life. If his brothers had been with him, they would have excused themselves and sought a lawyer of absolute competence. But he sat, hoping Ms. Eldridge would convince him to change his mind, that a divorce procedure would be too much bother for both of them.

"Now you must want me to justify myself," she said.

"No, no. It's fine," he said.

But she continued anyway, explaining that her own divorce had been so tangled that she ended up spending hours in law libraries tracking down precedents. She became fascinated, thankful that a disastrous marriage had let her discover her true interests. She ended up being more effective than the attorney she was paying two hundred dollars an hour. The irony, the wonderful poetic justice of it all, was that the settlement made her ex pay her way through law school. Before then she'd never earned a penny in her life, just bred children, three of them, and cooked and cleaned. And here she was a professional. She could hardly believe it.

Dale didn't know how to interrupt her. He kept crossing and uncrossing his legs, pulling his sleeve back from his watch and glancing down at the time. Finally, she realized.

"My God, I've spent the whole hour talking about myself. Listen, desertion is a piece of cake. I can't charge you. Come back tomorrow. Let me take you to lunch. I promise you won't have to hear any more about me."

"You're very interesting," he said.

When he came back she was waiting with her coat on, led him into the elevator, across the street to a restaurant. At the table she covered her mouth with her hands, wrote a note that she passed over the cloth: "You talk. I've taken a vow of silence."

He didn't know where to begin, and so started with the day he spoke to Gretchen outside the church. When he stopped it was two o'clock and he had not touched his food. He had never spoken for so long at one time in his life. "I must sound so foolish to you," he said, "allowing myself to live a life like mine."

"It's all right," she said and quickly slapped a hand to her mouth.

All the times he went back to her office he knew were unnecessary for his case. Ms. Eldridge explained from the first that a quick divorce was never in doubt. Yet he finally wanted to talk, to try to explain himself to someone, how lonely he had always been. "I treat you more like my analyst than my lawyer," he told her one day.

She smiled at him. "Then I should raise my fees."

The actual divorce hearing was a five-minute formality, Ms. Eldridge attesting that all attempts to find the deserting wife had failed. She and the judge exchanged words Dale didn't understand, and she whispered to him, "Let's go."

"Is it over?"

"You're a free man."

They went back to her office to sign papers, "to formalize the nonsense" as she said. She passed him forms and documents, X'd the line for his signature, and slipped each one in a folder when he handed it back.

When they finished, she reached into a desk drawer and brought out a styrofoam cooler. "I bought something to celebrate with. Your freedom, my first desertion success. It's only a California champagne because I didn't want to risk anything better in this refrigeration contraption."

Dale watched her untwist the wire fastener, tug at the plastic cork, and pour into two coffee mugs. "I should have done that," he said when she handed him his.

They clicked mugs and took sips. When she touched his shoulder and leaned forward to kiss his cheek, he met her eyes, set the mug on the desk, and kissed her mouth. When she embraced him back, he could feel the champagne from her mug saturating the back of his pants leg. They looked at each other and laughed. Dale had never laughed so hard in his life.

•

When Dale married Melissa, their children were all part of the wedding party, Joseph, Daniel, her son and two daughters. His brothers came from across the country with their wives; his parents sat in the front row. Most of the guests were her relatives and friends. At the reception Dale looked out in amazement at all the people who now filled his life.

He loved her; he was sure of it, the great joy he felt at having her beside him. "You've always been a nice man," she told him. "I'm so glad that I was the one to finally discover it."

Dale and the boys moved into Melissa's house, a sprawling rundown Victorian with cracks in the plaster and paint peels hanging from the ceilings. He expected Joseph and Daniel to resent the uprooting from the only home they had ever known, neighborhood friends. But from the time he explained that he would remarry, without a question or comment they went up to their room and began sorting through their belongings, each day lining another neat pile against the wall even though the move was several months away.

When they relocated, Dale never saw them apart, Joseph in the lead, Daniel a step behind, the two of them constantly climbing up and down stairs from the damp chambers of the basement to the huge unfinished attic where sunlight glowed through cracks in the weathered shingles.

Melissa's children, at home all their lives, raced in and out of rooms, slamming doors, cheering each other in a perpetual game. For hours each day, the house echoed with pounding and shouting and thumping. Dale hoped Melissa would scream for silence. When he finally spoke his anxiety, she laughed: "I read law books in this house; I'm oblivious to chaos."

"I keep waiting for someone to plunge over a bannister or crash through a window."

"What's made you so fearful?"

He described his sleeplessness after Gretchen was gone, waiting for the least sound from either boy, throwing back the covers and rushing to them as if they were suffocating.

"Don't you see that you all were suffocating before she left?" Melissa said.

Dale nodded. "It was my fault. My terrible loneliness. I made her a wife. A mother."

"Those boys are still afraid to breathe." She stood and moved to the doorway. "Joseph! Daniel!" Their names rang through the house.

When the boys appeared before her, Melissa knelt between them, reached out her arms, and hugged them with a squeal of delight. To Dale's amazement, they hugged her back, clinging, suddenly weeping. He had never seen his sons cry like this. Then he saw Melissa's children watching from across the room, and he stiffened. But when they met his eyes and smiled, he found himself crying too, standing tear-blinded until someone took his hand.

•

Although he lived only fifty miles from the city, it was unusual for Dale to go there. He disliked the traffic and the dirt and the crowded streets. But occasionally his company sent him for meetings that he dreaded.

This March day's meeting ran overtime; darkness had already fallen when he walked back to the terminal. A chill wind blasted through the alleys, and pinpoints of rain beat against his face. He turned up his collar and hunched forward.

At a street corner waiting for the Cross sign, he felt someone staring at him and glanced back at the woman under a storefront awning. When the sign turned green, he stepped off the curb, then wheeled abruptly with his recognition. Gretchen was still wearing the grey coat she had disappeared in ten years ago.

She was already halfway down the block, plunging ahead in a blind panic. Dale told himself he would continue on his way; he had nothing to say to her. But he found himself running after her, panting for breath moments after he began.

Now she was running too, tripping against cars stopped at an intersection. A burning tore through his lungs, a pain so great he wanted to clasp his chest and crumple on the sidewalk. But Gretchen was the one who fell, not twenty yards from him, suddenly losing a shoe and sprawling on hands and knees. He stumbled after and wrapped arms around her, trapping her in an embrace, gasping so hard he couldn't speak. He pulled her up and twisted her against a building.

"Why?" he finally said.

When he looked at her face, he saw drops of wetness magnified behind her thick glasses, tangled hair stuck to her cheeks.

"Why?" he demanded.

"It was all so awful."

"What?"

"Being me."

Dale realized how tightly he was clutching her shoulders and released her at once, then had to brace himself against the stone front of the building. He took deep breaths, drew the air deep inside him, lifted a hand to rub the rain into his face. Gretchen was watching him closely, as if she expected him to say something very important.

"The boys are fine." He forced himself to tell her. "They're very happy."

"I'm so glad," she said.

He turned and began walking toward the terminal, taking one slow step after another, refusing to look back.

Trap

The first thing Thomas noticed when the real estate agent drove them to the house was the boy next door, a handsome child of about five, barefoot, with short blond hair and tanned, well-formed legs. The boy followed the slow movement of the agent's Lincoln with vivid blue eyes, so solemn in his watching that Thomas smiled. He nudged Elena to make sure she saw him too. She had become distraught in the apartment, upset because their daughters, Jeanne and Nancy, three and four, had no playmates in the high-rise of retirees. Some nights she would embrace both girls and weep. Thomas expected her to be delighted at the sight of the child, but she just returned the boy's stare, turning her head with the passing of the car as if locked in contact.

When Thomas saw the house and yard, he knew it would be perfect, exactly what they wanted despite an asking price several thousand beyond their limit. Though the house itself was small, the location was ideal — the last home on a short dead-end street, opening onto a large field thick with wild flowers and bordered by a grove of towering trees. He could envision the girls tumbling on the lawn, running across the field, shrieking with joy.

"What do you think?" He wanted Elena to be as excited as he was.

"Do you know that boy?" she said.

"Of course not," he said, puzzled that she would ask.

•

When they moved in, Thomas followed the truck while Elena stayed back at the apartment with their daughters to make sure the movers missed nothing. He planned to set up the girls' beds and have their rooms in order before Jeanne and Nancy began their new lives, a camera strapped around his neck to capture their expressions.

The boy stood silently by a shrub close to the truck, watching the movers hoist boxes and dressers and overstuffed chairs out the sliding door in its side, dark men grunting instructions to each other, shirtless in the hot July sun. The boy seemed fascinated, not missing a thing, but breaking off twigs one after the other.

Thomas almost yelled at him to stop, then thought he was only a child, unaware of what he was doing. So to distract him he walked across the lawn and introduced himself, even shook the small hand. The boy stared down at the contact and then flinched away. Thomas had to ask him his name. "Davy," the boy said, flat, almost annoyed, as if Thomas should have known.

"I have daughters your age," Thomas told him. "Jeanne and Nancy. They'll be here in a few hours, and you'll all be good friends by the weekend."

Davy smiled and snapped off another twig.

•

All during the drive from the empty apartment to the new house, Thomas told the girls about Davy, calling him their new friend, suggesting the games they would play together. Each asked questions he couldn't answer — what toys the boy owned, his favorite cartoons, what he ate for breakfast. Thomas laughed and said they'd have all the time in the world to find out. Elena criticized the movers, sure they had stolen things, though she didn't have any examples. "We'll know when we unpack," she warned.

•

To Thomas's disappointment, Davy wasn't out waiting when they arrived. The car was gone from his family's driveway. But the couple across the street came down from their porch as soon as Thomas parked and the girls ran squealing to explore the house.

The couple was Stan and Betty Bergmann. Betty had baked cookies, assuming they would be arriving that evening when she saw the movers. Elena murmured "Thank you" five or six times, then almost dropped the plate.

The Bergmann's dog, a golden retriever called Aggie, leaped against Thomas, then shrank back at Stan's sharp "No," romping toward the girls, licking one face and then the other. They clung to her and giggled.

"She's wonderful with children," Betty reassured Elena. "Ours grew up with her."

"What ages are they?" Thomas asked eagerly.

"Chuck is ten and Liz twelve. A little too old for your girls."

"Well, they'll have Davy."

Thomas was struck by the Bergmann's sudden silence, the quick glance they gave one another, the immediate tautness in Elena beside him.

Stan knelt beside the dog, scratching ears as if it were something that had to be done with great concentration. "Davy's a bright boy," he finally said. "But a bit rough for girls."

"What do you mean?" Elena stared at him.

"He's a very physical child," Betty said.

"How?"

"He doesn't know his own strength some times," Stan said.

Betty twisted a button on her blouse. "He pushed Liz down the stairs."

"But she's twelve," Thomas said.

"On purpose." Elena made it more statement than question.

"Oh no, it wasn't like that," Stan and Betty said quickly.

•

The next morning Thomas and Elena slept late, exhausted from the move, not waking until Nancy cried for juice and they opened their eyes to bright sunlight. He was taking a few days of vacation to unpack. Elena let the girls play outside but insisted they stay close to the house.

As he hung curtains in the master bedroom, Thomas could see them standing against the side of the building watching Davy in his own yard, just as still, looking straight back at them. Then the boy did a series of perfect cartwheels from the front of his house to the back and then out to the edge of the road. The girls laughed out loud and ran inside to tell their parents.

It will be all right, Thomas told himself. By tomorrow Jeanne and Nancy would be tumbling beside him, not nearly as coordinated, but having great fun all the same.

•

After dinner, the house in order, the unpacked boxes stacked against a wall of the basement till the weekend, Thomas opened a bottle of cognac, took the good glasses from the sideboard, and poured drinks for Elena and himself.

"Here we are," he said and reached out to touch her glass in a toast, relieved when she finally smiled back, charmed by the twists of hair that had slipped loose from her headband while she worked.

From the yard he could hear children's voices, his daughters talking to Chuck and Liz from across the street, their words lost in the whir of the ceiling fan, then later Davy, louder than the others, telling how he had climbed all the way to the top of a tree.

When he realized it was silent outside, he relaxed with the thought that the girls were being watched by the older children, that Liz would soon be their sitter, first for an hour or so in the afternoon and eventually for long evenings when they visited friends' homes or drove into the city.

He was sprawled on the sofa, drifting on the edge of sleep, Elena' dozing beside him, when a frantic banging shook the side door, Jeanne screaming with breathless gasps. Elena leaped awake, and he followed close behind, thinking that the door was unlocked, wondering why Jeanne didn't just turn the knob, expecting to find the child splattered with blood. But when Elena threw back the door, he didn't see a sign of injury, just one girl's distorted face and her sister's wailing.

Elena swept up Jeanne and then Nancy. "What's wrong? What

happened?" Elena kept asking, her voice cracking with panic. Jeanne just shrieked. He carried Nancy into another room, stroking her hair, nuzzling her cheek with his stubbled chin, a gesture that always made her laugh. She responded with a mixture of sobs and giggles.

"Did Jeanne get hurt?" he said.

She nodded vigorously.

"How?"

"Davy did it."

"Did what?"

"A stick."

"What with a stick?"

Nancy poked a finger at her eye.

When Thomas went back to Elena and Jeanne, the child was still hysterical, her face squeezed shut when he tried to look. Finally, he spread the skin apart with two fingers and saw a small scratch at the edge of her eye, just a fraction of an inch from the socket. There had been almost no bleeding, and he was sure her screams came from fear, not pain.

Later, when the girls had settled down in their beds, Elena kept insisting, "It's what the Bergmann's told us. He's dangerous."

Thomas nodded. "We should talk to his parents. Work out some rules of how they play together."

"I don't want my daughters near that boy."

"They're neighbors. Kids have fights and then make up. The girls do it all the time. Davy has to realize girls can't roughhouse."

•

At breakfast Elena warned Jeanne and Nancy to be very careful with Davy, to call for her at the first sign of an attack. But by mid-morning, while Elena rearranged the bedroom closet, Thomas looked out and saw the three of them sitting in a circle on the lawn, arranging stuffed animals, lifting them one at a time with squeaking high voices as if they were puppets. He told himself he could delay talking to Davy's mother until after lunch and wondered how he would approach

103

a woman he had never met with a complaint about her son.

•

The woman's name was Peggy Ann; her husband off somewhere at work was Art. She was already out in the yard weeding her garden when Thomas approached along the road, a short darkly tanned woman, thick-legged in shorts, the remnants of a pretty face in leathery skin. She met him with a friendly greeting, introduced herself, and apologized for not coming to him and Elena. "We've been so busy," she said.

They spoke of the greenery, the abundance of the neighborhood. She had been born in her house, received it as a gift from her parents when they retired. She seemed to know each tree and shrub individually, remembered them from the day they were planted, those in his yard as well as hers. She named the families who had lived in his house for the past thirty years, identifying them by their changes to the landscape. Thomas had the feeling that she thought of them all as transients, people just passing through and that she already considered him and Elena and the girls temporary.

At last, sure Elena had been watching him the whole time, standing back from a window, hidden behind the sun glare, he made himself bring up Davy. "I've met your son."

"Yes." He could see her smile tighten.

"A good looking boy. He looks like a natural athlete."

She relaxed. "He has my father's coordination."

"Has he told you about my daughters? Jeanne and Nancy?"

Peggy Ann looked down, fixed the strap on her sandal. "He did mention that there were children next door."

"They're not used to playing with other kids. No one else in our apartment building had any. They don't know any little boys." He hesitated and then blurted, "I guess things got a bit rough yesterday."

"Davy said everything was fine." She threw back her shoulders, clenched the garden shears.

"There was almost an accident, a twig poked near Jeanne's eye."

"Sometimes he gets overtired. He'd been up half the night before.

He needs his sleep."

"Could you tell him they're only little girls? They're not fighters. He's a very intelligent boy. I'm sure he'd understand."

"Davy isn't cruel, just rambunctious."

Their parting was pleasant. Peggy Ann was back to talking about the garden, but Thomas was sure she would say nothing to her son.

•

Things went well till the weekend. The girls had been giving most of their attention to Liz, who enjoyed the mother role, though Thomas knew that wouldn't last. Davy stayed at the fringe of group, participating in some games, hanging back with derisive noises during others. But Saturday afternoon Nancy was in tears, not nearly as frantic as Jeanne had been about her eye, but still a very unhappy child.

"Davy threw sand in Nancy's face," Jeanne announced, both outraged and smug at being the bearer of the news.

Thomas was ready to be amused. Kids were always throwing sand, but Elena's distress upset him. She got up and left the room, her eyes red, mouth open, as if she were on the verge of gasping.

"I have to talk to that women," she told him later, after dinner, while the girls were in their sleepers watching a Disney video.

"I tried," he told her.

"Not enough. You should plead with her. These are our children." Her voice was raised; he expected her to begin ranting. But she gave him an odd look and turned away.

•

Thomas pretended to wash the porch railings while he watched Elena confronting Peggy Ann, unsmiling, her posture rigid. Davy's father, Art, was at his garage workbench; every now and then Thomas could hear the shrill rasp of a grinder.

When Elena returned, she seemed satisfied. "I was very direct. I told her I'm sure her son is hyperactive. I know the symptoms. There are medications, behavior modification therapies. She'll thank me if he can be straightened out before he starts school."

•

But Monday morning as Thomas began the drive to work, Peggy Ann dashed out in front of his car, blocked the street, waving arms, pounding the air with a fist. "Tell your goddamn wife to leave my son alone!"

"She was trying to help. She knows a lot about the subject."

"There is no subject. Davy is perfectly all right. Your wife is a lunatic."

She kicked a sandal against his car door, and Thomas sped away before he said something cruel, not sure if he should tell Elena, trying to imagine how it was going to be to live in this neighborhood for years to come.

•

When Thomas returned from work, no one was home. "I took Jeanne and Nancy for a picnic," Elena told him when she got back a half hour later, while he was still searching through the house for a note.

"We walked forever and ever," the girls said.

He wanted to reason with Elena, stress that she couldn't hide every day, then realized that she must have seen Peggy Ann in the street that morning; she was spending hours at the windows just looking out at the neighborhood.

All through dinner, the Bergmann's Aggie barked endlessly, the girls imitating, first one and then the other, laughing harder and harder. When he saw Elena grimacing as if she had a terrible headache, Thomas yelled at them to stop and cursed at the dog.

After they ate, at sundown, while the girls were taking their baths, Thomas decided to walk in the yard. When he stopped to admired the hydrangeas, he noticed the basement windows behind the bush were broken, all the glass missing from both frames, except for a few jagged edges. He hurried to the back of the house, then to the other side. Every window was the same, deliberately and carefully destroyed. When he looked up, he saw a small face staring down at him from a bedroom of the house next door.

He expected Elena to be furious, but she merely nodded as if she had known all along. "We have enemies," she said.

"It's only a child."

"He's not alone."

•

Thomas tried to talk to Art, strolled into the man's garage as he was hammering a sheet of metal clamped in a vise. He casually mentioned what had happened to his windows, knowing he couldn't accuse Davy directly.

Art, a wiry bald man with a smooth pointed face, slammed the metal with a rubber mallet. "That's the problem of living at a dead end close to the woods. It invites trouble."

"Is there a lot of it?"

"Now and then."

"Who do you think did it?"

"Teenagers." Art snipped off a corner with a metal shears.

•

The next morning Thomas found long deep gashes along the driver's side of his car, a circle etched below the front door handle. He had worked late the night before, came home after dark, and couldn't believe Davy would be out at that hour.

"I guess it really is teenagers," he told Elena.

She shook her head. "I saw him."

"When?"

"Past midnight. I couldn't sleep."

"Why didn't you say something? Stop him? Get me?"

"It wouldn't do any good." Her eyes were dull; he had never seen them so lifeless.

"Of course it would. I'd have saved the car and gotten proof to show his parents."

"They don't care. They sent him." Her voice was flat, expressionless.

But Thomas was agitated, furious at the boy, angry at her passivity. "Listen! They've got a real problem — a four-year-old prowling in the middle of the night. We've got a problem."

•

Peggy Ann slammed the door in his face when he rang her bell. Art ignored him in the garage. Stan and Betty were noncommittal. "Davy's always been a difficult child. Peggy Ann dotes on him. She had three miscarriages. She spent half her pregnancy with him in bed. She can't have any more." "Doesn't she want him to grow up normal?" Thomas insisted. "It's hard to talk to her," they said.

•

This time there was blood, streams of it flowing from the top of Nancy's head, down into her eyes, blinding her, gathering in a thick line on her neck as if her throat were slit. Elena screamed and screamed. Thomas had to shake her, shout at her to keep quiet, so that he could help the child.

When he examined it, he knew the wound wasn't serious though it would need stitches in the emergency room, a tetanus booster, a patch shaved from the top of her head. He pressed a towel to the cut, abandoned Elena and Jeanne to their crying, and carried her to the car.

Two hours later, on the way home, reaching up a hand to touch the thick bandage, Nancy told him what happened. "Davy hit me with a stick."

"Were you fighting?"

"No. Me and Jeanne was playing."

"You mean he just walked up to you and starting beating you on the head?"

She nodded. "Is Davy a bad boy?"

"Very bad. You and Jeanne should stay away from him." Thomas wondered how they could hide in their own yard, why they should have to.

He had called from the hospital to reassure Elena, assumed her responses of "I see, I see" meant that she would be calm when he and Nancy came home. But her found her sitting in the middle of the floor, chin on her knees, rocking back and forth with grinding teeth, Jeanne tugging at her shoulders, trying to make her stop.

Thomas lifted Nancy in his arms and shouted, as if in triumph, "Here's the brave girl," hoping his wife would smile. But she didn't look up at them.

•

Stan and Betty nodded sympathetically at the story, terribly sorry at what had happened.

"I'm thinking of suing," Thomas said casually, eager for their reaction.

The Bergmanns drew back and looked out toward the distant trees. "I wouldn't if I were you," Betty said.

"Why? Parents have some responsibility."

"The people before you tried that," Stan said.

"I thought their children were grown."

"They had a cat."

Thomas's first reaction was not to ask for the details. But he had to know.

"She was a sweet thing," Betty said. "Liz cried for days. Even Chuck."

"What happened when the people sued?"

"You have to remember that Peggy Ann was born in this town," Stan said. "Everybody liked her parents. They were oldtimers."

"Is that why the people moved?" Thomas asked. "Why we were able to buy this house?"

"There were lots of reasons," the Bergmann's said.

"What about Aggie?"

"She's a big dog. She can take care of herself."

•

"I don't like you talking to them," Elena told him.

"Stan and Betty? They're on our side."

"They only pretend to be. Don't trust them."

Elena wouldn't go to bed. "I have to be on guard." She spent the night drinking pots of coffee, sitting in a chair by the living room windows, staring into the darkness, indignant when Thomas pleaded with her to stop.

He expected her to be exhausted, to collapse in the middle of the day. But a strange energy seemed to burn inside her, an obsession with vigilance. When the girls played outside, she stood over them with a furled umbrella, glaring in the direction of Davy's house. Every time Thomas drove up and saw her, he found her pose ludicrous but didn't know what else either of them could do.

When he tried to discuss the problem with her, she shook him off. "I have a plan" was all she would say. They ate in silence, rarely shared the bedroom, the only conversations in the house between his daughters.

•

One evening Thomas drove home to find eight-foot sections of a stockade fence spread out flat on the lawn, thick posts already planted in the earth. He walked about his yard, threading in and out of the fence sections, touching toes to the points of wood, wondering if the weight would kill the grass.

"I ordered it," Elena told him, smiling for the first time in weeks. She handed him the work order and the bill.

When he saw the cost, he dropped into a chair. "We can't afford this."

"It's our only choice, the only way to save ourselves." She was shaking her head in a frenzy, her eyes glistening, her hair wild.

He looked from the bill to her face, hoping she would finally be able to rest, that a long deep sleep would make her herself again.

•

By the next night the fence was up, six feet high. From his car Thomas couldn't see the shrubs or the windows of the first floor. It's ugly, he thought. As he got out of the car, he heard Jeanne and Nancy giggling behind it, and he wanted to cry.

He stood looking for a gate, a handle he could open, and wondered if it would be locked, if he would have to shout for admission.

Something tugged as his arm, sudden and fierce. He turned to Peggy Ann standing in the road, her face livid. "What have you done to my home!"

"Privacy," he said, the first word he could think of.

"This is my where I live!" She was ranting, her cheeks quivering, and he saw her as an old woman, haggard and jowled, her expression fierce. "You've made my home horrible!"

"You know the real reason," he said, more frustrated than angry. "Your son attacks my daughters. He destroys things and hurts things."

Peggy Ann slapped his face. For an instant Thomas thought he would hit her back. But he did not move and repeated. "Hurts." She slapped him again and turned to stomp back toward her house.

•

Thomas didn't like being downstairs, glancing out a window and looking directly into the tight strips of the fence. Even upstairs his bedroom faced Davy's house, the silhouette of Peggy Ann pacing behind the picture glass. He preferred to stay in the girls' rooms, taking turns from night to night, reading stories until Jeanne or Nancy drifted into sleep, then sitting with the light off to look out toward the shapes of the trees in the moonlight, knowing that Elena was in the darkness below, legs crossed, frantically jiggling a foot as she waited for something to happen.

•

Thomas could tell the Bergmanns were annoyed by the fence, considered it an eyesore, though neither said anything directly. It was the way Betty shot sideways glances at it, the questions Stan asked about cost and construction, how long Thomas thought it would last. "Until Davy goes to college," he said; but Stan didn't laugh.

He hated the fence himself, shocked at the sight of it every night when he returned from work. People, friends in the office, asked when they would see his house, and he made excuses, ashamed to let anyone know the way he was living, afraid to bring Elena into company. Each new day, when he came down in the morning, he expected to rediscover his wife, hear her greet him with I'm all right again and smile, like someone recovered from a harrowing fever. But whenever time he saw her she looked as if she had been locked in a dungeon for years, pallid, gaunt, eyes haunted.

•

The calls started soon afterward, in the middle of the night, ringing and ringing, Elena an arm's length from the receiver refusing to touch it, even when Thomas pleaded. He would rush downstairs to answer, bellowing, "Tell me who you are," at the silence and then cursing. Five minutes later the ringing would start again.

The third night, past 3 a.m., he dialed Peggy Ann's number, ready to shout "Stop it" and hang up. But the boy answered on the first ring — "Hello, this is Davy" — as if he had been waiting. Thomas was stunned. Had his mother put him up to it? Did she even know?

After Jeanne woke up crying the fourth night and set her sister off, he unplugged all the phones from the jacks before he went to bed.

It was quiet for a few days. Then the noises began, loud slams against the side of the house that would jar Thomas from his sleep. Elena sat unmoving, but the hand with the cup trembled, splashing coffee into her lap. Thomas waited till daylight to search the yard for the object that made the noise — a rock, a slab of board — but found nothing.

•

Elena started to pace, up and down stairs, along the hallway, peeking into each girl's room. Thomas could hear the creak of boards, the squeak of hinges, the patter of slippers.

One night she opened his door, and he closed his eyes, waiting to see what she would do. He felt her approach, her breath against his face, something muttered into his ear.

He sat up and snapped on a lamp. "What? What?"

She seized his mouth in her hand, clamped the jaw shut. "Ssssh! Whisper," she hissed.

"Why? What's happening?" He spoke as softly as he could.

"They're all listening."

"Who?"

"Peggy Ann. Art. The Bergmanns."

"How? Why?"

"Microphones hidden all over the house. Planted before we moved in. The lightning rod is a transmitter."

"Why should they want to? We hardly say anything."

"They're after our children. They want to steal them from us."

"Kidnapping?" Thomas felt foolish asking questions, having this conversation, as if he were locked in a weird ritual.

"Or death." She burst into tears and smothered her sounds in the blanket, stuffed a corner into her mouth until she gagged.

•

Elena wouldn't allow the girls in the yard unless she or Thomas stayed with them. One Saturday he watched their quiet play, the passing of dolls from one to the other, when the first stone landed near his shoe. Then more stones followed, a rain of them, pebbles, gravel, handfuls sprayed over the top of the fence and scattering on the grass.

Jeanne and Nancy watched in fascination until Thomas sent them inside and opened the gate to the street. Davy stood with stones in each hand, a child's pail of them at his side. The Bergmanns were watching from their dining room, Liz and Chuck too, ducking back when they realized he had seen them.

"Davy!" he shouted.

The boy stared defiantly, even as he approached, even as Thomas lifted the pail and dumped it into the grass. "No more of this. Go home."

The boy swung both arms, tossed handfuls of stones into Thomas's face, stinging his flesh, then planted his feet and stared. He was daring Thomas to strike out, and Thomas was the one who fled, afraid of his own rage.

•

"It's not his fault," Elena whispered. She was always whispering, muffling her words with a hand cupped at her mouth.

"How can you say that?"

"The others have done something to him. He can't help being what he is."

•

Sunday Thomas tried to read the paper as he sat in a lawn chair beside the girls. But he couldn't focus; nothing happening in the world — wars, floods, famines — mattered any more.

When a section of fence started to shake, he thought he was hallucinating, until it moved faster and faster, the posts wriggling in the ground. Then he saw the two small hands clinging to the points at the top, rocking back and forth.

Jeanne and Nancy hadn't noticed. They pretended to plant a garden, squealing over imaginary flowers that were so beautiful. Neither could say the word without stumbling over a syllable, but kept using it again and again.

It's going to come loose, Thomas thought. He's going to pull the fence down. It struck him that the others must be watching too — Peggy Ann, Art, Stan, Betty — witnesses at a strange spectacle.

When the fence section gave way with a groan of nails, Thomas shouted. Davy rushed into the yard carrying two sharp rocks, bearing down on the girls. They tumbled to the grass, covering their heads with their arms, already wailing.

Thomas rose and planted himself in front of them, lifting the lawn chair, ready to crash it down on the child, not caring if he were maimed or killed. He had never felt such raw hatred.

But before he could act, Elena ran from the house and dropped to her knees, wrapping both arms around the boy, pressing her face to his, wild with weeping. "We're prisoners!" she cried. "They've made us both prisoners!"

For an instant, Thomas thought Davy would smash the rocks on her head. But the boy let them fall from his fingertips. He clutched back at Elena, face twisted, crying just as frantically.

Fathering

"I just got fired," she told the man suddenly standing next to her across from the beer taps, a stranger she would come to know as Carson.

First thing that morning Murtaugh had summoned her into his office to unfold the new organization chart and point out the missing block where her name should have been. Her slot, he explained, had been eliminated in a budget cut.

Now it was 10 a.m., about the time everyone else was in the middle of a coffee break, but Gerri had slammed the door on Murtaugh and driven straight to the four-stooled bar tucked into a corner of a neon-lit package store. She never drank, had barely sipped the glass of chablis, but couldn't think of anywhere else to go.

"They wouldn't call it that," she continued, even though the man hadn't turned to acknowledge her. "The company never fires anybody. Murtaugh claims I'm surplus."

Carson spoke to her reflection in the mirror. "Maybe he meant above and beyond."

"Sure. Beyond hope."

He slid onto the stool beside her, the only other customer at that hour, dressed in a neat blue business suit and bulky white turtleneck.

"Anybody else would have gotten a transfer," she told him. "But they've already tried that with me. Murtaugh was my third boss this year. They say I've got an attitude problem."

"Do you?"

"Who wouldn't, having to put up with that bunch of losers? Murtaugh didn't even have the balls to fire me outright. I get a RIF package. A year's salary and medical benefits."

"Now you've got twelve free months to indulge yourself." Carson gave her a thin smile.

Gerri couldn't tell whether he was joking.

"I want to indulge myself by working."

"That's because you don't know any better yet."

She looked up at the bar clock. "Why are you here? Did some asshole fire you too?"

"I only work when I want to."

Gerri swiveled her stool and looked at him closely. He was a tall lean man in his forties, not bad looking, with a face like a V — broad forehead tapering down to a pointed chin. If it hadn't been for the pouches around his eyes, he could have passed for much younger, her age. "Where do you get a job like that?"

"Have a rich father."

"Sure. You just call home and he ships you money."

"It's more secure to have him keel over from a myocardial infarction when you're 22. Then it's all just sitting there for you to draw out at your pleasure."

"How's your heart?"

He lifted Gerri's hand from the bar and slipped it under his lapel. "Feel any problems?"

His ribcage thumped against her palm. A quiver went through her groin even though his type didn't appeal to her. She pulled her hand away. "I'm not a doctor."

"But I am," he said. "Just like my dad."

"Bullshit. I've never seen a doctor hanging around in bars at ten in the morning. Shouldn't you be in a white coat peering up somebody's insides?"

"I didn't say I practiced medicine. I just have the degree. It was something my father dreamed of. He died a month after I graduated. So much for my medical expertise."

"I thought you said he died when you were 22."

"I did."

"That's when people get out of college, not med school."

117

"Not me. I finished college at 18."

"That'd make you some kind of genius."

"No. I'm just clever at certain things." His mouth pressed down in a tight line.

•

He introduced himself as Carson, then bought her a split of champagne to toast her liberation. "Life's too short to be a slave to work."

She twisted the glass on the bar top, wouldn't lift it. "Work is what people do when they don't have a rich father."

"And what sort of a dad did you have?"

"A drunk." Gerri tried to say it casually, making her voice tough, the way she always did five minutes after she met someone and relieved her compulsion to reveal the truth about her father, as if any conversation with her had to be based on that essential information. "Not a fall down, slobbering, violent drunk," she explained even though Carson had given no indication that he wanted to know. "He was a gentleman drunk who sat rigid in a chair and told everybody how much he hated living."

"When did he die?" Carson asked.

"He didn't. My mother did. The last I heard he was worried that he was cursed with eternal life."

"Not what you'd call a close family."

"I call my sister once a year."

"Then you're the next best thing to an orphan. We're two orphans floating on the breezes of life."

"You're a little too old to be an orphan," Gerri said, annoyed because he didn't shake his head and say how awful it must have been to have a father like hers.

"That's what my children tell me," Carson said, "whenever I remind them how lucky they are to have a living father."

"And what does your wife say?" She clutched her purse under her arm and slid to the edge of her seat.

He locked a leg through the rungs of her stool. "Wives. All

former."

"You must be a treasure to live with." She tried to stand but found herself trapped by his knee.

He shook his head. "Great fun to drift with. Some can stay in the current longer than others. But they all have very pleasant memories. We relive them when I visit my children. Isn't the world a better place when you're with yours?"

"I have no children."

"Husbands then."

"There was only one. And that was so long ago it probably never happened."

"You decided he was surplus."

"Maybe it was the other way around."

"Did he think you have an attitude problem?"

"He was no different from everyone else."

"I really think we should celebrate the first day of your wonder year."

"We?"

"Call it a lesson in liberty from a master."

Gerri blinked and expected him to disappear. But there he was, in the mirror, still gazing at her with a crooked smile.

She looked at the clock again. Only fifteen minutes had passed since she walked through the door. "Why not?"

•

Gerri drove home to drop off her car, Carson following in his black Continental. She wanted him to wait outside her apartment while she changed from her office outfit, but he insisted on coming in, charging up the steps ahead of her, offering to help pick out what she'd need.

"For what?" she demanded, tempted to clutch his coattails and drag him down.

"You never can tell."

She hesitated at the door, keys dangling from her fingers, ashamed of the mess within. "I'm not a neat person," she told him.

Inside, Carson ran a finger through the dust on the coffee table. "Cleaning up might be a waste of time."

"Why?"

"You could decide to abandon everything and run off with me for a fascinating year."

"To do what?"

"Meet my children."

She forced a laugh. "I could do that in a day or two."

"It's not that easy. I've got progeny from coast to coast. Florida, Oregon, Texas, Illinois, California. Some are always on the move — like me. I have to track them down."

"So I should spend a year with you hunting for your runaway kids?"

"They're not lost. It's just a matter of being in the right place at the right time. Coordinating schedules."

"And what would they say about me?"

"They're open to any possibility. Just like their dad."

Gerri took in the shambles of her apartment — piles of plastic garbage bags, pots stacked in the sink, newspaper taped across the windows because she had never gotten around to buying shades. If Carson hadn't been there, she would have sat down and wept. Behind his narrowed eyes, she was certain, he was reading her mind.

He touched her shoulder. "Just grab a toothbrush."

Gerri moved into the bedroom, and Carson hovered in the doorway while she packed.

•

When they approached the entry ramp to the interstate, Carson stopped at the fork between eastbound and westbound. He lifted a stack of maps from the console and fanned them like playing cards. "Pick one," he told Gerri.

She folded her hands in her lap.

"We need a destination," he said.

"I thought we were visiting your kids."

"But which one first?"

"Whoever's closest."

"Too easy. I prefer surprises."

"You're crazy. We'd be wasting thousands of miles going back and forth."

"Usually the most pleasant journey between two places is a zigzag."

Carson rippled the maps under her nose. When Gerri slapped at his arm, he let the maps flutter to the floor mat. "Illinois is on top," he said. "We start with Nola."

Gerri told herself to open the door and get out while they were stopped. She closed fingers on the handle and felt his eyes on her hand. But he said nothing, just sat there with the engine idling and the car in neutral, as if daring her to leave. When she brought her hand back to her lap, he eased onto the westbound ramp.

They drove with only the hum of air conditioning. The monotony made Gerri doze. When she opened her eyes to the dashboard clock, it was after 3 a.m. "When are we going to stop?"

Carson smiled at the windshield. "I'm rarely ever tired." He pulled out the ash tray, and she saw that it was crammed with capsules. Without looking, he pinched one between thumb and forefinger and brought it to his lips. She watched his Adam's apple swallow. "The best part of being a doctor," he said, "is the prescription pad."

"What if you have a bad reaction?"

"I have a wonderful constitution. Everything agrees with me."

•

At dawn he pulled off the highway into the parking area for a motel. "Do you want to eat before or after we sleep?"

"I don't have any appetite," she said despite the hollow in her middle.

"After then."

In the room Carson went directly to the shower. Gerri realized she had left her suitcase in the car but was too tired to go back outside. Without a nightgown, she dropped her clothes into a heap on the floor and slid naked between the sheets.

She could barely hold her eyes open, saw the room through a blur of lashes. When Carson came out of the shower, he was wearing a pair of bikini briefs that accentuated the pallor of his hairless body. His arms and face and neck were deeply tanned, but the rest of him was a pasty white. While his shoulders were broad, he had no dimension from front to back, thin legs protruding buttockless from his trunk.

Even though he did not attract her, Gerri pressed her hands between her thighs awaiting his approach. From the moment he sat next to her at the bar, she knew there would be sex, just as well now than later so that she could learn to adjust her private pleasures. But he lay atop the covers, reading a book, separated from her by the thickness of blankets.

•

"You'll like Nola," Carson said. "Everybody does. She's the least intelligent of my children, but the sweetest. It's not that she's dumb, just that her siblings test off the charts. Fortunately, she suffers no complexes about being average."

"How old is she?"

"Nineteen or twenty. I can never remember."

"And what does she do?"

"Assistant manager at one of those fast food chains. McDonald's, Burger King. I can't remember that either."

"Then obviously you don't mind your children working. Their father hasn't given them a life of ease."

"There's only so much inheritance to go around. Part of my incredible good fortune in life was being an only child. Even if I were inclined to share with my progeny, the money would be too diluted to make anyone happy."

"You could do a lottery like the maps. Put all their names in a hat and pull out one to get it all."

Carson shook his head. "I only like games I can't lose."

He didn't phone; they just appeared at the counter while the girl stood behind the grills scrubbing a deep fryer. Carson ignored the boy who asked for his order and called out, "Nola, it's your father."

She rubbed hands across her apron and ran out to embrace him. "Daddy!" The customers stopped in mid mouthful to stare up at the scene. Nola was a strapping girl with wiry red curls and a freckled pug face. Cute, Gerri thought, as if looking into a pet shop window.

They sat in a booth, Nola squeezing her father's hands between hers and repeating, "This is great, this is really great."

"You're looking terrific, sweetheart."

"This is wonderful, Daddy."

Carson introduced Gerri and Nola reached over to shake hands, gazing at her father the whole time.

Carson and his daughter spoke of so many names Gerri gave up trying to sort out relationships. Fragmented doings of Mark and Harriet and Tom and Valerie and Janet and Bud and Katie. She hoped a customer would insist on service and shut off the girl's gushing enthusiasm.

"Hey," Carson finally said. "We'd better be moving on and you'd better start turning out burgers before people starve to death. We wouldn't want to be responsible for a famine in southern Illinois, would we, Gerri?" He stood and gestured that she should follow.

"Come back real soon, Daddy."

"Tell your mom hello for me."

"I will. She'll be sorry she missed you."

Nola kissed him and then pressed her face to the window as he guided Gerri across the parking area.

From the lot all Gerri could see was the two-lane highway and acres of dried corn stalks in every direction. "Where in the hell are we rushing to? This one's supposed to be your sweetest kid."

"Nola knows I love her."

"Even if she is tedious, she deserves more than a hit and run visit."

"Couldn't you see how thrilled she was?"

•

They had crossed into Missouri two hours before, a half tank of gas still left, Gerri desperate for him to stop. She was sick of being sealed inside that car, breathing the odor of new leather, clutching and unclutching the padded handles.

Carson broke the silence. "Tell me about your dad."

"You already know as much as you need."

"Do you hate him for being a drunk?"

"Why are you so interested?"

"I'm a father too."

"Not like him." Gerri looked down and saw that she was knotting the front of her blouse in a fist, so tight she had popped a button.

"How am I different?"

She didn't believe he really wanted to hear but told him anyway. "He's the way he is for a reason."

"He's a statistic. There are thousands like him."

"I only knew one."

"The source of your attitude problem."

"Goddamn you! It's not a joke."

"Everybody needs a dad."

"Not some bastard who won't let you be normal. Who made you grow up hating yourself!"

She burst into tears, furious with herself for crying, pressing her face down against her knees. Touch me, you bastard, she kept thinking, hungry for Carson to reach out a hand and stroke her hair.

•

They drove most of the day every day, Carson pouring over maps and circling places with interesting names. Despite his hours of monologue on each of his children — Dwight, Maura, Sean, Mark, the twins, and the rest — they were hardly fifty miles closer to any of them with all the back and forth to the places he picked. One was no different from the others, small towns of white frame houses that seemed rooted into the ground like the ancient trees that spread above them. Each time they drove onto a new row of settled streets, Gerri tried to pretend that she was going home, about to climb onto one of the broad porches, open a door, and step into a room where people would embrace her. That would be Carson's surprise, the reason he had come for her in the first place. But he never stopped, and she always reentered the highway with a sting of disappointment, cursing herself for prolonging the fantasy.

●

There still wasn't any sex although he paraded around nude after his evening shower, penis always flaccid, even after she began tossing the sheets half off, exposing a leg or a breast. He would meet her eyes, give her one of his odd little smiles, and stay shrunken amid the pubic fuzz.

Gerri felt no desire. His pallid nudity made her queasy, as if she had to watch a flayed creature every night. But, finally, when he moved beside her and snapped off the light, she turned on him, furious for his lack of arousal, cursing him in her head — Bastard! Bastard! He lay inert until she whispered, "Please," then suddenly pulled her so tight she couldn't breathe.

Later, when Carson lay sprawled beside her, inches away from touching, Gerri said, "Why did you wait so long?"

"I've been looking for a sign."

She knew that from then on whatever satisfaction she received would be a confusion of pleasure and rage.

●

In Beaumont, Gerri met the fifteen-year-old twins, Krysta and Kyle. She and Carson unpacked their luggage in the guest room of a ranchhouse that seemed to sprawl for acres. "How can we stay here?" Gerri wanted to know. "I'm still half-owner," Carson told her. "And besides, Joycelyn wants to talk finances."

Joycelyn shared a huge master bedroom with Rafael, a courtly man with a charming musical accent. He and Carson would sit up all night sampling rare South American wines and sharing memories of cities they had known at different times. Joycelyn carried a brown strong box, trying to make Carson go over the papers locked inside — deeds, receipts, title insurance. But he shook her off, engrossed in Rafael's words. Joycelyn barely acknowledged Gerri, except for abrupt nods when they passed in a hallway.

Carson and Rafael took to jogging together each morning. Gerri wouldn't leave the house. Every time she opened the door she stepped from the air conditioning into a wall of sizzling humidity and inhaled a cloud of yellow pollution.

Kyrsta and Kyle were both flunking ninth grade, Carson told her, despite having the highest IQs in the district. They spent every spare hour designing video games. He seemed amused by their weirdness.

They took to seeking out Gerri in the family room and guiding her down to what they called their lab, a corner of the basement crammed with monitors and disk drives. Whenever they made her try one of their games, she always did something wrong that sent strange shapes flitting across the screen.

"What's Carson really like?" they asked one afternoon.

The question startled her. "You're his children."

"We don't see him that often. You're with him all the time."

"He can drive for hours without saying a word."

"Do you love him?"

"I hardly know him."

"No matter how hard he tries, he can't make himself lovable, can he?" Krysta said.

"The sad part," Kyle said, "is that he wants so much to love us."

When Gerri and Carson left, Joycelyn and the twins didn't come out to the car to say goodbye. Only Rafael kissed Carson on both cheeks, Gerri on the mouth.

•

Carson didn't bother to consult his maps now, just flipped coins at intersections and swerved the big car in sudden turns. After two solid days strapped onto that seat, watching him swallow a pill an hour, staring straight ahead in head-throbbing silence, Gerri began beating the dashboard and pleading, "Let's get some place!"

"Hey, we've got the rest of the year," he told her. "I don't have enough kids to fill up that many days."

"Carson, how many goddamn children do you have?"

"That depends on the criteria you use. Known to the courts or unknown. Legitimate or illegitimate."

"I thought you had all those wives."

"I did. But there were others in between. During."

"The grand total. All categories."

"Including the unclaimed ones?"

"What does that mean?"

"Take the one I call Carson Junior who thinks he's really Carl, the son of a man named Roger and full brother to his siblings. So does Roger, who believes in the sanctity of marriage. Even his mother works hard at denying I ever existed. Though every few years I call — out of the blue — to ask about our son. It makes her weep."

"What an awful thing to do."

"But I weep too. Just think of it — a son I've never known. Who's never known me."

•

"He abducted me once," Gerri said to the darkness. It was the middle of the night, now and then a semi passing by on the highway and sending vibrations through the windows. From the rhythm of his breathing, she could tell Carson was awake beside her. "I was eight."

"Abducted you from where?"

"Our house."

"You can't abduct your child from your own house."

"From my bed. I woke up and felt the mattress shaking. There he was leaning over me with that thick, sweet breath of his. 'Get up, get up,' he was saying. Then I heard my mother shriek in the hallway."

"And you were sure someone was dead." Carson yawned and arched his back.

"Yes."

"But nobody was."

"He made me stand up and pulled a dress over my head, twisted my arms into the sleeves. All I could think was, why didn't my mother come in the room to help."

"State of shock."

"When he turned on the light, I saw how terrible I looked in the mirror. All twisted and disheveled. He tried to brush my hair, but his hands were trembling so much he just made knots. Then he picked me up and carried me past my mother. 'At least my daughter's not ashamed to be my escort tonight,' he told her. When he got to the front door, she finally said something."

"'I'll kill you, you bastard. That's what my wives always end up saying."

"'At least put on her coat, for God's sake!'"

"But he didn't."

"He dropped me onto the front seat of the car, and I was too frightened to be cold. When he backed out, he scraped cars parked in the street. I'll never forget how loud that metal sounded."

"Where did you end up?"

"A bar. He sat me on a stool, ordered a Coke, and joined a crowd of people who seemed to know him. They were pointing at me and laughing. Some woman came up and kissed me on the cheek. She tried to wrap her arms around me. When I could see past her, my father had disappeared. I couldn't find him in the middle of all those people. I'd never felt so tired. But I was terrified that if I fell asleep, he might forget I was there."

"Did you ever get home?" Carson said.

A great bubble swelled in her chest, and Gerri thought she would smother from within. She had to gasp for breath. "Not yet," she finally said.

•

Gerri watched purple neon flash against the edges of the blinds in a motel outside Anaheim. Carson sat silently in a chair, a position he took the moment they entered the room. She was waiting for him to unbutton his jacket, move his suitcase from the doorway.

"We're only four hundred miles away," he suddenly said. "Maybe it's time I got a look at Carson Junior."

Gerri sat upright. "You can't be serious."

"I've never laid eyes on him."

"Don't you understand how cruel that would be?"

"He's my son."

"You haven't cared about him in eighteen years."

"I care about all my children. I never forget I'm their dad."

"What about his family? You'd ruin their lives."

"Why should you care about them?"

•

They sat parked on a winding street of brickfront homes and bright flowering shrubs. Under a bright blue sky and sparkling sun, it was a very pretty neighborhood. People were barbecuing, children squealing from backyard pools. Gerri studied the houses, wondering which would have been hers if she were someone else.

People were looking at them, a man and a woman inside the only stopped car on a street where every home had a double driveway, space for visitors. Gerri wondered if someone would call the police. She imagined an officer trying to make Carson move on, knowing he could make an accomplice of any policeman in five minutes.

Even with the windows down, the strong sun heated the car until Gerri felt that she was suffocating on stagnant air. "Maybe they're away for the weekend," she said. "Can't we go?"

"No hurry. We've still got most of your year left. Carson Junior has been waiting all his life."

Even though she watched the minutes change on the digital clock, she couldn't keep track of time, unable to stop imagining how it would feel to be that boy.

Then Carson clapped his hands. "There he is." Gerri looked up and saw a tall youth emerge from the side door of the house across from them. He had Carson's build, Carson's face, more the image of him than any of the other children she had met.

She clung to his arm, wrestling his hand from the door handle. "Please. You've seen him. That's enough."

Without taking his eyes from the boy, Carson shook her off and spoke very softly. "There's something you don't understand."

"What?" She was trembling, twitching her head, afraid to hear.

"There's no way to hide from your father."

Gerri squeezed her eyes so that she would not have to see. She heard Carson slam the car door and cry out, "Son!"

She curled on the seat, rocking back and forth, too weak to scream, knowing from the moment Carson reached out to embrace him that boy would despise his life.

Handyman

Douglas had been living in Alicia's house for two months — early June to early August — when the boy forced open the front door with his shoulder, stumbled into the foyer, and dropped a huge duffel bag on the marble floor. His slight body twitched in a spasm of surprise when he saw the man towering above him. Douglas was wearing only underwear — tee shirt and boxer shorts — sliding his white socks over the smooth, cool surface as he crossed from the circular staircase back to the kitchen. His first reaction was to think that the duffel bag was bigger than the boy and then to wonder what this boy was doing there.

But the boy asked him first. "Who are you?" Green eyes wobbled behind thick lenses, the mouth scowling, brown hair matted as if it hadn't been washed in days. He looked about twelve, narrow-shouldered, legs rickety in khaki shorts, both knees crusted with yellow scabs. What struck Douglas most were the great round glasses halfway down the freckled nose and the oversized white sneakers on his feet.

Douglas looked down to compare his own legs with the boy's, and saw that they were lean and muscular from the work he did, blond hairs glowing in the sunlight that streamed through the open door. His body often surprised him, the solidity of it, evidence that he occupied space in the world. He was a tall man, his angular face covered with a week's growth of beard, the fair hair on his head sparse, even though he was not quite forty.

"Who are you?" the boy demanded again, the high voice cracking with a tone of outrage.

"I'm Douglas." Amused, puzzled, he reached out a hand that the boy ignored.

"What are you doing in my home? Where is my mother?"

"Alicia!" Douglas called — hesitantly, swallowing the sound, unsure that he had the right to raise his voice in this house. She was always the one who shouted at him. In fact, she was constantly shouting, berating him or someone else, the men who mowed her lawn or serviced her BMW, most often her sonofabitch bastard of an ex-husband. But in all her hours of ranting and rambling, she had never mentioned a son.

"Alicia!" he called again, louder, when the boy seemed about to scream.

This time she answered. "Hold your goddamn horses!" The voice, he knew, came from the third level, where she spent a good part of every day sorting through papers locked in fireproof cabinets shoved under the eaves.

He looked down at the boy. "She's coming."

The boy gave him a withering you-idiot glare.

Douglas fixed his gaze on the stairway, silently cursing Alicia for not appearing immediately. After several minutes, hearing only the rapid snorts of the boy's breathing, he spoke. "Been with your father?"

"Him! Hah!"

I could, Douglas thought, go back up to the bedroom and put on my pants. Or continue into the kitchen where he had been heading in the first place and pour a cup of coffee. Leave the hallway to mother and son for whatever reunion they would have. It was no business of his. Yet he stayed, surprised that he was annoyed with Alicia for keeping this child a secret from him. Not that she owed him anything. He still wasn't sure what he was to her. From the very first weekend he slept in that house, he had been expecting her to end each outburst by slapping his face and demanding that he get out, immediately. And yet she never did.

His irritation bothered him. He didn't allow himself to have emotions. His mantra was, keep calm, keep calm. No matter what happens, keep calm. As far as he knew from nearly forty years, all emotions could do was fuck you up. Things happened. But he tried never to be the cause. Even so, things were always happening, and when they did, he just sat tight and waited for someone else to respond. Alicia ranted, and he just nodded, even though he knew his lack of a reaction infuriated her even more. But if he did respond, even with a gesture, there was no telling where that might end. No, the best thing was to bear her temper and enjoy what there was to enjoy — the steaks, the wine, the cigars, the heated pool, the handling of the BMW. All that was good, very good. He'd hold onto it as long as he could.

What the coming of this nasty, four-eyed little twerp meant, he had no idea. He wouldn't think about it, not yet. Perhaps the boy would hoist that duffel bag, stagger under the weight, and disappear. Wouldn't that be nice?

Yet he heard himself calling once more, "Alicia!"

And there she was, suddenly appearing on the landing, halfway up to the second floor, an odd-shaped woman, as narrow as her son above the waist, but bloated below, her backside swelling against bright red stretch pants. Every time he saw her again, Douglas thought of a gourd. Still, she was very rich and clever enough to have kept all the money and all the property after the divorce. "That sorry bastard didn't get a pot to piss in." She said it daily; it was one of the few things that truly gave her pleasure. Douglas had never imagined there could be a child, didn't even think to ask.

"Mother, who is this fool?" The boy was pointing at Douglas with cramped little fingers. Douglas resisted the urge to slap them away.

Alicia pulled herself up, her haughty pose, sweeping one hand over her shoulder. "This, my dear, is Douglas. He does chores around the place."

"I know what kind of chores you have him do. It's disgusting."

"It's none of your goddamn business."

The boy made a gagging noise, then stuffed fingers down his throat and stamped his feet.

"Oh, stop it," Alicia said.

The boy became still, immediately. "I could report you to child welfare. This isn't a fit home."

"Good. Your father would get custody. It would serve you right. You'd have to cram all your books into that pig sty."

"There are sties and there are sties," the boy said.

Alicia descended to the hallway, barefoot — she never wore shoes and socks indoors — her toes clenched on the cool marble. "Dougie," she said. He started at the name. She never called him that; she never called him anything. "Dougie, I'd like you to meet my son, Zachary. Zachary is a child prodigy, a certified, tested, off-the-charts IQ phenomenon. Not that it does him any good. He's a rotten little snot."

The boy lifted himself to tiptoe, his nose still no higher than his mother's chest. "And what is Dougie?'

"Dougie is a craftsman."

"Dougie is a human dildo. That's what I'll call him. Dildo. Mr. Dildo. Sir Dildo. Dougie the Dildo." The boy began dragging the duffel bag up the stairway, straining as it thumped after him one step at a time.

Douglas didn't know if he was supposed to help, but decided it would be a mistake to offer. He felt relief that the boy hadn't insisted that his mother kick him out.

"Zachary," Alicia pretended to be telling Douglas, but looking at her son, "has spent the summer at a camp for geniuses. He's probably come back a super genius."

"You didn't tell me you had a son." Douglas tried to keep the displeasure out of his tone.

"I didn't think it was important."

"It would have been nice for me to know."

"Oh. So I suppose I should let you know I have a daughter too."

"Is she in genius camp too?" Douglas asked, picturing a Zachary clone with shoulder-length hair.

"Hardly. She's a wacko. In the loony bin. Though they'll be releasing her any day now."

Douglas swallowed. "And then what?"

"She'll come here. Back to the room with gashed walls. The one I keep locked." She had told him it was for storage, crammed with useless junk.

"I could have replastered."

"No point. Some things are beyond repair."

"Is she a threat?" Douglas didn't like danger. He told people he was an orthodox coward, unembarrassed at the admission.

"She hasn't killed anyone, if that's what you mean. Not yet."

●

Alicia had called Douglas at the end of May, before Memorial Day. His name was in the Yellow Pages, just a line of plain type. He couldn't afford more, not bold face, not a display block. She needed some work done around the house, a bit of plumbing, some electrical fixtures, a few rooms papered, and he advertised himself as someone who did general repairs, a handyman.

"How did you find me?" he asked her the first day, curious why someone with a home so large, so far back from the road, surrounded by woods, with swimming pool and tennis court, would pick him.

"I opened the book, closed my eyes, and jabbed with a nail file. There you were, right under the point."

He scanned the property and saw weeks of projects, odd jobs that would get him through the summer. Walking through the house with her, he pointed here and there at some things that might need touching up — a loose fixture, a crack in the plaster, a creaking floorboard. Nothing blatant, nothing that would seem like grasping for work. He spoke offhandedly, almost implying that none of it really mattered, that it was all optional. The strange thing was that was how it had ended up, him prowling the house all day trying to find things that would keep him busy, she never giving him a cent. But he had excellent food, fine cognac, Cuban cigars, a bed with satin sheets, use of an elegant automobile, and a pool with a Jacuzzi.

When Alicia called, Douglas hadn't had work in several weeks. He was almost living in his car, a twelve-year-old station wagon with bald tires and a rusted exhaust system, the back strewn with tools, paint cans, drop cloths, odd pieces of pipe, and rolls of wiring. By then, his landlady had locked him out of his apartment — really just a room with a hotplate — and he spent some nights at one of his sister's forty miles away. But they had never been close, and her husband had disliked him for years, but now openly, insultingly, sneering with executive disdain, as if Douglas were low life.

The odd thing was that the man had been a fraternity jock, partying every night and barely graduating, while Douglas had made dean's list twice in his three years of college. Yet he didn't go back for his fourth. It wasn't money; he had a scholarship, and good grades required little effort. With an aural memory, all he had to do was pay attention in class and write out what he had heard in bluebooks. But the whole thing seemed pointless, just words about things that didn't matter. He stayed on with his summer job assisting a general contractor, while his parents had a fit. Then they got used to it, Douglas — aside from the few months of a marriage — living in his old room till he was past thirty, eating dinner with them occasionally, usually out in a diner as if he were a boarder. When his parents died, the house was sold, the small profit split among his siblings, and his share just seemed to disappear. He liked fine brandy, expensive cigars.

And Alicia didn't begrudge him. He could drive the BMW into town and put things on her tab. Merchants never batted an eye, as if theirs had been an arrangement of longstanding.

The first time he arrived on the property, he had parked off to one edge of the circular drive, aware that it would be inappropriate to bring the battered station wagon any closer to the house. When he saw Alicia, waiting for him, standing under the portico, he was struck by her odd shape, almost repulsed at the incongruity of her body halves, as if she were some sort of freak. And now they slept in the same canopied bed, she straddling him almost every night, making strange grunting sounds that got louder and louder until she clenched all her muscles and seemed to levitate. During the day, they never spoke of it. In fact, they had little to do with each other beyond her haranguing at mealtimes, she off with her papers, he prowling about the property trying to make himself useful.

•

The daughter, Jordan, appeared as suddenly as Zachary. But this time Douglas was out in the garden clipping dead vines from a trellis when the white van pulled into the drive. As soon as he recognized the icon of a wheelchair on the side panel, he knew exactly what was happening. For the days since Zachary's arrival, since he learned of the girl's existence, every time he passed the door of the unseen gashed room, he paused, then hurried past, as if a sudden shrieking would assault him.

In bed, Alicia a mound beside him, small sputtering sounds emerging from her lips, he would stare up at the ceiling and imagine the girl's madness, picturing someone witch-like tugging at great knots of tangled hair, wrists gnarled with the scars of slashings, wild eyes fixed, mouth gaping. And he would shudder, his calves cramped with the sudden quivering of his legs. Instead, the girl who emerged from the van — young woman actually — stepped lithely on the stones of the drive, wearing a white dress with a billowing skirt, her lustrous dark hair fixed in a French braid. She moved with an air of tranquility, though Douglas suspected it must have been medication. She wasn't really pretty, but she had a pleasant face, perhaps the way Alicia's would have been if it weren't clenched in a perpetual knot of outrage.

Douglas surprised himself by stepping out from the garden to greet her, offering to shake, then realized that his hand was coated with soil. Still, she squeezed it between her thumb and fingers, and then looked with wide expectant eyes.

"My name is Douglas," he told her.

"I'm called Jordan," she said. Then, still touching his hand, she asked, "Do you live here?"

That stuck him as odd. Anyone would have thought he was just a man working in the garden. "For now," he answered.

"I live here sometimes myself. And then I live other places."

"Are you glad to be home?"

"It never lasts."

The fingers tightened on his hand, thin as they were, hurting him. He wanted to pull away, but feared she might cry, the way she stared at the ground with her face rigid. Then he noticed the attendants who stood beside the van, a man and a woman, both in white, both short and plump. They stepped toward Jordan, ignoring Douglas, one on each side of her, each taking an arm and leading her toward the front door, pulling her away from him until the contact was broken.

The door opened from the inside. He expected to see Alicia emerge to greet her daughter. But it was Zachary rushing out to hug his sister, lifting her off the ground though his head only came to her chest. "Zachary," the girl said, very softly, as if making a sound of wonder.

•

The boy, it turned out, was fifteen, not twelve, and a junior in a local college, majoring in philosophy, driven back and forth by a man who looked like a retired banker. Douglas saw him once when he came to discuss his arrangement for the fall with Alicia. She hadn't introduced Douglas even though he had to walk through the room twice to retrieve tools he stored in the panty.

Now, with several weeks before classes began, Zachary seemed to spend every minute with his sister, reading to her much of the day, usually from works of philosophers like Aristotle — the Nicomachean ethics — and Spinoza or novelists like Stendahl and Robert Musil. The high childish voice rang with enthusiasm, clearly enamoured with the sound of words and the rhythm of sentences. Douglas had a vague memory of some of the books from his years in college, and though he had grasped them well enough to get B's, they didn't mean anything to him, just a puzzle to decipher, like fitting a new valve. Jordan, on the other hand, didn't seem to understand at all, merely gazing at her brother, eyes lowered, head bobbing, as if mesmerized by the flow of words emerging from his lips.

Douglas wanted to ask Alicia about the girl's madness, why someone apparently so passive had to be locked up. Were the walls of her room really gashed? But, of course, he didn't. He never initiated a conversation about anything beyond another need for repair. Alicia, however, was different with the girl in the house. The days Zachary had been back without his sister, nothing changed. The boy spent all his time reading in a room far down the hall, too distant to hear her night noises. Yet when the girl was in the house, Alicia didn't sleep, talking half the night, never about the girl, always about the father. She hated the man, growing more and more agitated as she spoke of him, often just saying his name — Brian — over and over and pounding the mattress with her fist.

Douglas began to piece together a story. Brian always claimed to be traveling for business. He was never home. He may have had mistresses. He wrote large checks to cash. He even owned a condo in Florida that she knew nothing about. As much as he could understand why any man would want to avoid a wife like Alicia, he suspected that the real reason was Jordan. Even though Alicia never gave a clue, Douglas felt certain the man had run from the girl's madness, perhaps from both a crazy daughter and a weird genius son. Children nothing like children were meant to be.

Douglas avoided the siblings as much as possible, creating projects outdoors despite the August heat, new cedar shingles on the gazebo, a replacement filter for the pool, stone borders around the flowerbeds. He found himself thinking of his own son, a boy he hadn't seen in years, fathered not long after he dropped out of college during his one brief marriage. Marie had pursued him, had even been the one to propose, though she put the words in Douglas's mouth and, as he knew the moment he spoke them, believed they were coming from him. The boy, Donny, had been adopted by his stepfather and now had two half sisters. They all knew it was useless to come after him for support. The day she left him, his soon to be ex-wife had said, "Don't worry about that. You can't even support yourself." For a short time, he sent Donny cards for his birthday and holidays, then gave up because there was never a response. And he felt relief. But now he kept thinking, at least he's normal.

As much as he had feared what the meals would be like with Zachary and Jordan in the house, Douglas needn't have worried. Zachary prepared a tray from the serving dishes on the table and then took it off to his sister's room. He expected Alicia to protest, yet the most she said to her son was, "Don't forget the asparagus."

Douglas could enjoy the food without stress, and he did relish the cooking of the woman Alicia called Martha, though that wasn't her name, a shriveled old Asian women well under five feet, who — to his knowledge — spoke no English and spent all her time in the kitchen or in her small sleeping quarters adjacent, a space no larger than the pantry. Her name did begin with an M sound, and she voiced it every time Alicia addressed her as Martha. But Douglas couldn't comprehend it either. For all her wonders at a stove, she might have been a kitchen machine. She never acknowledged anyone, and they didn't feel it necessary even to say hello to her when they entered her area.

Alicia had no taste for the brandy that he craved after each dinner, swirling it in one of the elegant snifters from the shelves of crystal. She did sit with him, rattling on about the people who had offended her in her life, though she seemed to have no human contacts off the property. The phone rarely rang, and the only time she picked it up was to call a lawyer or a broker, abrupt, conveying an order without pleasantries.

She did insist that he smoke his cigars outside. He would sit for an hour in the screened gazebo hearing the sizzle of insects against the bug zapper, the rustle of animals in the woods. This was his favorite time of the day. Some evenings he would take one last swim in the pool. When he went back inside at twilight, Alicia would be playing dissonant music, strange jagged sounds erupting like sparks from hidden speakers. He never asked who was making the music, and it pained him to listen, though he sat with her until it was time for bed. He didn't think she owned a television; at least, he never found one in any part of the house that he had seen. He would have liked to watch a program, any program.

•

Some days Douglas thought Jordan was following him. He would look from wherever he was working, under a sink or the top of a ladder, and find her staring at him, arms rigid at her side, like a soldier standing at attention. He would smile and say something like, "How are you, Jordan?" She never answered, and he felt uncomfortable, dropping tools, hammering a finger, until he heard the slap of Zachary's footsteps running in the hallway. The boy would take his sister's hand and guide her away, not even glancing at Douglas.

Then, after several weeks passed, it was time for Zachary to return to college. One morning, his driver, the retired banker, showed up with the boy's class schedule and sat for an hour with Alicia in the library, entering each period on a large monthly calendar. Several days later the man returned with a sack full of books, Zachary pasting his printed nameplate in every one, carefully aligning until it was centered on the page. Douglas was outside at the time, on a ladder, re-hanging a paneled shutter and looking in though a window. Jordan stood in a doorway, watching, a hand at each shoulder, tugging at hanks of hair with clenched fists.

From then on, he noted her growing agitation — mismatched shoes, sweaters on backwards, smears of lipstick across her cheeks, on her forehead. She wasn't eating, Zachary returning untouched trays of food to the kitchen several times a day. He would see the boy, gripping his sister's hands, whispering in soft urgency, a look of pain on his face.

Douglas wondered if he should say anything to Alicia. She rarely referred to her children, at least not in the present, only in the past, one night carrying a box of baby toys down from the third level to the bedroom, spreading them across the mattress. "This was Jordan's favorite doll. This was Zachary's teddy bear. He loved this little toy car. She wouldn't let go of this Pooh Bear." It reminded him of reminiscing over the possessions of a dead person, the two times he and his sisters sorted through belongings of a deceased parent.

When the sex stopped, Douglas realized she knew the state her daughter was in. He felt sure she didn't want him to make the first move. So, at midnight, when she turned off the last light, he stretched out on his back, absolutely still, and waited for something to happen, awake half the night as she thrashed back and forth on the mattress.

•

At twilight one evening just before Labor Day, Douglas came in from his nightly cigar and found Zachary and Jordan in the foyer, the girl huddled in a ball on the marble floor, knees drawn into her chest, hands gripped around her ankles, as she rocked back and forth. The boy

141

was pleading: "I'll take you with me. I promise." Douglas imagined what it would be like to sit in a classroom with a crazy woman in the next row, in the seat behind him. A crazy woman and a shrunken little genius. It wouldn't be fair to the others, the normal people.

Zachary spoke louder and louder: "I'll take you! I'll take you!" And the girl began moaning, a harsh open-mouthed animal sound.

Alicia emerged from the library. "You both know that's impossible. You're different people. You have different lives."

Douglas had never heard her speak this way, calmly, gravely. For a moment, when he saw her haunted eyes, he felt sorry for her. He almost made a gesture to step toward her when Jordan sprang up and let out a shriek, screaming and screaming as she ran from wall to wall of the foyer, beating fists against the gilded mirrors, kicking the banister, heaving her body at the door with great roaring grunts.

When she ran into the dining room, Zachary was at her heels, Alicia frozen with her hands in the air. Douglas followed. The girl threw open the doors to the china cabinet, lifting armfuls of dishes and hurling them down to the floor, scaling serving plates into the windows, a din of crashing. Within seconds her brother was following her, imitating each act of destruction. If she gouged the table with a silver pitcher, he gouged next to her mark. If she swung a serving bowl at the chandelier, he swung one too. Then she reached for the crystal goblets, snapping off the stems and raking her bare arms with the jagged edges, long lines of blood swelling over her pale flesh. Zachary hesitated. Douglas saw him swallow. But he picked out a glass and cut himself, cringing at the first wound, and then did it again.

The old woman called Martha appeared. Perhaps she had been there all along. Douglas hadn't seen her at first. She was standing in the doorway to the kitchen, wizened, like a mummy in a bathrobe, watching dispassionately. He sensed that she was guarding her territory, her things, that if the brother and sister made a move for the kitchen, she would block their way with a great force in her tiny body.

Instead Jordan ran back out into the foyer, up the stairway, Zachary two steps behind. Now the noises were loud and echoing, the scraping of furniture across a floor, the tumbling of large wooden objects. A minute later, Alicia moved, taking the steps slowly, one at a time. Douglas stood below as she went into the bedroom they shared and shut the door.

What did she want him to do, he wondered. Go to her? Use his strength to stop her children? He put a foot on the stairway, then turned abruptly and stepped outside into a sultry evening. He hadn't realized how humidly unpleasant the weather was, how artificially the central air had cooled the house.

His shoes crunched over the stones of the drive as he walked toward the garage. It had gotten dark. Behind him, inside, every light was bright. Shadows rushed past the windows on the second level, from room to room and then back again, glass shattering, broken objects dropping onto the grass, onto the stones behind him, chair rungs, bedposts, a drawer front, scraps of fine wood ornately carved. Many times he had run his hands over the smooth finish, tracing fingers in the grooves, and envied their craft.

In the garage, Douglas's old station wagon sat parked next to the silver BMW. He hadn't driven it in weeks and wondered if the battery was dead. The door hung heavy when he swung it open, dragging on the hinges. He had to force upward on the window frame to pull it shut. It had been that way for at least a year. Back inside the house, all his clothes were stuffed into a dresser drawer, his good toolbox in the pantry, but that didn't matter.

He reached a hand under the seat for the ignition key. He always put in there, in every car he had owned for the past twenty years. His fingers groped across the carpet, a wider and wider circle, his wrist strained. No key. For a second, he considered getting down on his knees and searching with a flashlight. But he knew what had happened. Had she hidden the key somewhere in the house? Or had she thrown it away, out into the tangled brush beyond the shrubbery?

There were ways to start a car, wires to twist and spark. He had done it. Many times. Electricity was one of his skills as a handyman. But then he thought, where would I go? He pulled up his feet and stretched out across the bench seat, his head propped on the armrest. He closed his eyes, expecting, eventually, to fall asleep, fingers reaching through a tear in the plastic upholstery, probing the dry foam rubber padding as if to find an object he had lost. In the morning, he knew, someone would have to clean up the mess, begin the endless hours of repair. Tonight he missed his cigar.

Ten Years

It mortified Philip that he despised Arthur Weigant so much. Such loathing shamed him, as if it were a severe flaw. He never revealed the emotion to anyone else in the office, not even at home to his wife, though he found himself grinding teeth in the middle of the night when an image the man invaded his thoughts.

The aversion began one morning ten years ago during the brief period Philip had reported to Arthur after joining the corporation. The scene haunted him like a foul taste he couldn't spit out. Arthur had given him a mediocre performance evaluation, checking "average" in every category, and Philip — disbelieving — had confronted the man in his office fully expecting a retraction, an apology. "I've always gotten superior ratings," he said, embarrassed to be defending himself. Arthur had leaned back in his chair, propped scuffed shoes on the edge of a wastebasket, and said, "You're nothing special. You'll never be." Despite the rage surging within him, Philip turned, walked out, and closed the door slowly, softly, thinking I hate you, I hate you — the words resounding in his brain for days.

Philip had never asked anyone why, but the evaluation never harmed his career. In fact, he received a promotion a few months later, as if Arthur Weigant's opinion was of no importance. Still, he considered it a stigma festering in his personnel file. He wondered how the company could put up with a man like that, a man who contributed nothing and destroyed morale, why he hadn't been fired.

Now he and Arthur were peers, Arthur transferred to a branch office in another state, their contact minimal — names copied on the same distribution lists. But tonight they were booked into the same hotel for a three-day conference, Philip just minutes from home, staying over because everyone had to be available for late sessions. On occasions like these — annual meetings and the like — when forced to be together, Philip always managed to sit at the opposite end of a conference table or the other side of a dining room and rarely looked in Arthur's direction.

•

That was why Philip kept wondering what he was doing in the hotel bar with the man, straining to make conversation in a noisy room, desperate for a long shower and a deep sleep.

Arthur had stopped him in the lobby after an early evening workshop and invited him for a drink, suddenly linking arms and steering him toward the bar. Philip had wanted to shake him off, but it would have been like a wrestling match in front of the company's other managers. So he nodded at familiar faces as Arthur pulled him through the open door.

On a stool beside Arthur, swiveling back and forth, gazing up at the ceiling lights, Philip realized that he knew nothing about the man's life. Because others were watching, he knew he couldn't appear rude. Yet he didn't know what to say beyond platitudes about the company's plans for the year, shouting over the clamor of voices in the room. Arthur just nodded as if nothing he said mattered.

Infuriated by Arthur's blank expression, Philip was about to demand what the man wanted. Before he could speak, Arthur moved closer and touched Philip's arm, thin fingers clawing the sleeve of his sweater: "I have a favor to ask. I'd like you to do something for me tonight."

"What kind of favor?"

"Pick up my daughter and bring her back to the hotel."

Philip sat back, pulled his arm away. "I don't understand. It's your daughter."

"You live nearby, know the area," Arthur replied.

"You did too once."

"A long time ago. Things have changed. I'll probably get lost."

"Then I'll draw you a map."

Arthur picked up his drink and stared down at the bottom of the glass, rocking the ice cubes back and forth: "I don't know how she'll react to me. I haven't seen my daughter — Angela — in ten years."

"My God!" Philip pictured his own children, three school photos on his desk, thinking how much he missed them when he had to be away on business, like now.

Arthur clenched his glass, so tight his fingers trembled. "It was a brutal time. That's why I begged for a transfer. I'm still furious with her mother."

Philip realized the man was contorted with anger, his face flushed, his suit jacket wrenched askew, his collar digging into his neck. He felt his own pulse throbbing with distaste. Just as he was about to rise and leave, Arthur swiveled directly in front of him, blocking his path.

"You're probably wondering, why tonight, after so long?" Arthur said. "It's because she's going off to college soon. She'll finally be away from that woman. Now it's time to know my daughter."

"Then just go to her."

"I'm afraid. That's why I'm asking you. She doesn't have any reason to hate a stranger."

"Hate you for what?"

"Things were vicious before I left. And then I ignored her, never even sent a card."

His hands were squeezing the glass so hard it seemed about to shatter, pierce them both with fragments. He talked, on and on, about the marriage, about the child, about his anger and frustration, about all that he had lost. The man was in pain, but Philip scorned Arthur Weigant's suffering.

"Why did you give me that evaluation?" he blurted.

Arthur looked stunned. "What are you talking about? What evaluation?"

"Average." His throat constricted at the word.

"When was this?"

"Ten years ago."

"For God's sake! My life was falling apart. I probably wasn't even thinking about you."

"You had no right. My life has nothing to do with yours."

"I don't remember. If I did it, I'm sorry. Please. I need your help now." Tears spilled from Arthur's eyes. His face seemed about to collapse, and Philip was on his feet ready to turn his back, about to say, softly, quietly, Never.

But just at that moment, a large man approached them, grinning broadly, reaching out to shake hands, the vice president both Philip and Arthur reported to. "I didn't know you two were friends." Arthur was smiling back at him. "Oh, yes. Years. Philip was about to do me a personal favor. For old time's sake." He crushed a piece of paper into Philip's hand as the vice president slid onto the vacated stool. "Don't let me stop you," the man said.

Philip burned to strike out, smash his fist into Arthur's face. Yet he did nothing but leave the bar.

•

And now he was the one lost, at sea in a neighborhood that seemed a clone of his own three towns away.

Philip drove slowly, looking for signs, house numbers, watching lamps brighten in the windows, illuminating rooms of soft furniture, wall mirrors that reflected quiet comforts. Everything looked familiar, the architecture, the trees and shrubbery, the sweeping green lawns, but here he didn't know where he was, what he was looking for.

The address lay on the passenger's seat, scrawled on the hotel stationery that Arthur had forced on him, the ink smeared from wrinkling. Even with the name of the cross street, Philip couldn't find the way. He circled around to the same intersection three times, then shouted curses, furious at being there, doing this service for a man he abhorred.

It struck him that he could go back and tell Arthur there was no such address, no such house, no such person. He wouldn't be believed, but that wouldn't matter, not when the man he lied to was Arthur Weigant. Still, he parked at a corner and unfolded the map from the glove compartment, turning the paper in his hands for the right perspective. Frustrated, swearing, he wouldn't quit now, as if this search were a puzzle he had to solve, a trial to prove self worth.

Arthur couldn't even describe what Angela looked like. She was eight the last time he had seen her, a skinny girl with toothpick legs and long black hair twisting loose from a braid. She wouldn't cut it, no matter how much Arthur demanded, no matter how much he told her she looked like a slob. Her mother had defended, hugging the girl to her side, shouting back at him, glaring defiantly, violent quarrels that had nothing to do with a child's hair. She chose her mother, Arthur had told Philip: "All this time I couldn't forgive her for choosing her mother. When I moved out, I told them I'd never talk to either one again."

Philip swerved abruptly at a corner and found himself on the street he had been seeking all along. A house mid-block was brightly lit, a bulb over the front door, an electric lantern casting a wide circle on the lawn. This had to be it. He pulled hard on the wheel to turn into the driveway, then changed his mind and edged to the curb, as if he had no right to park on this stranger's property.

He sat in the car, lights out, engine off, realizing that his hands were sweating, drying them across the front of his sweater. He swallowed, cleared his throat, hesitant to get out, as if he were the man who had disowned a daughter, not someone with a wife and children five miles away, a good father. "This is crazy," he said aloud and pushed open the door.

As he walked up the path, he watched for the drapes to part, eyes to peer from the front window, but the cloth did not move. Standing on the front steps of grey slate, he poised his finger over the docrbell, breathed deeply, and pushed. He heard chimes, the resounding of three rich notes, then footsteps and the thud of a twisted bolt.

He expected to stare into the eyes of a dark-haired girl, a young face burdened with the enigma of her father. But the woman who answered was middle-aged, attractive in a silk blouse and beige wool slacks, her neat square features set off by the crescent sweep of gold earrings. Philip thought his wife had identical earrings, was sure of it. The woman didn't speak a word, just stood there clutching the door as if unwilling to let him inside.

Philip didn't know what to call her. Mrs. Weigant? Did she still use that name. Had she remarried? He sensed a man's presence in the room, a shape that moved past an alcove. He met the woman's eyes, ready to recoil from a glare of malice but found only uncertainty. He understood at once that she was not the ex-wife, not the girl's mother, not even someone who had ever seen Arthur Weigant. And this was the woman's house. The mother didn't want Weigant in hers.

"I've come for Angela," he said.

The woman pulled back the door. Philip waited for a gesture to enter, then stepped into a hallway without one, startled when an orange cat darted past and disappeared behind the sofa. He scanned the living room, the rich wood of the tables, the framed prints on the walls, the Persian carpet on a bare bleached floor. When he glanced up, the man stood center in the alcove, tall, grey-haired, wearing dark flannel slacks and a sweater, just as he was. "Angela?" Philip said, looking this way and that, wondering if he had come to the wrong place.

A slight girl appeared on the stairway, the clothes hanging from her — jeans, a sweatshirt, battered running shoes too bulky for her feet. She moved down slowly, clutching an oversized canvas purse, hesitating, one step at a time, clinging to the banister. Fear in her eyes, a hand at her throat, she twisted the neck of the sweatshirt. Now her hair was close-cropped, fluffed, ends jagged, the way his own daughter wore hers. The style wasn't becoming to either of them.

When the girl reached the last step and stood across the room from him, Philip saw the tears in her eyes, the trembling of her shoulders. "Angela?" he asked even though he had no doubt.

Her voice quavered. "Are you . . . are you my father?"

The question stunned him, and then he realized that he and Arthur shared a vague resemblance: the same age, the same size, the same coloring, glasses, balding in a similar pattern, faint echoes of one another. He was being mistaken for the last person on earth he would ever want to be.

But here, amid strangers, he shocked himself by thinking, of course, and speaking aloud, "Yes," startled by the sound of his own voice.

150

At that instant he wanted to invade Arthur Weigant's life, to dispossess the man he hated. He repeated, deliberately now, speaking to himself as much as to the girl, emphasizing the words: "Yes, I'm your father." Philip had the sensation that he had stepped into a dream, as if anything that happened during this night would vanish in the morning. But when he met Angela's eyes, he tensed, wondering what would happen next, half expecting to be struck down for the lie.

The girl's face collapsed. She turned and ran back up the stairs. Philip could hear the creak of springs as she threw herself on a bed, then the deep misery of her sobs.

The man and woman converged on him, forcing him back against a wall. "You bastard," the man swore. The woman looked about to spit in his face.

They were releasing emotions Philip had felt for years, but now he felt compelled to defend himself, as if they were accusing him and not the other. "This isn't my fault," he said. With a simple "Yes," he had assumed the burden of acts he didn't even know.

"It's certainly not hers!" The woman pointed up the stairway, furious.

"You must be friends of her mother," Philip said, realizing that he didn't even know the ex-wife's name. The woman nodded, an abrupt jerk of her head. "Then what you've gotten is just one side. You don't know what it's like to be me."

"There's no excuse for what you've done."

"And what do you think that was?" Philip suddenly craved information, clues that would help him be someone else.

The woman sputtered outrage. "You had no right to deny that child," the man insisted.

Philip imagined his own children standing in that room, rejected, eyes begging for his attention, as if he had not spoken to them every day of their lives, calling each evening when he had to travel, once from Singapore, from the other side of the world, confusing time zones and waking the family in the middle of the night. "I wrote," he claimed, though he knew Arthur hadn't, because if Angela were his daughter he would have. "Her mother must have destroyed my letters."

"I don't believe you," the woman said. "She wouldn't do such a thing. As much as she detests you, she wanted Angela to have a father."

"She has one," Philip insisted. "A person can't not have a father."

"You're about as little of one as I've ever known," the woman said.

Philip noticed wood-framed photos on a table under the window, young people in their twenties who must have been this couple's own children. Their expressions were radiant. "I'm here now," he said with a sudden urge to repair Arthur Weigant's damage, to make right what that man couldn't.

He heard a creak on the stairs and looked up to see Angela descending slowly, one step at a time, wiping her tears on the sleeve of her sweatshirt. The woman moved up to hug her, much taller, cradling the girl's head against her shoulder. "Tell me, honey. What do you want?"

"I don't know." The girl wailed the words, miserable.

"Do you want to call your mom?" the man asked.

"Yes." Then the girl shook her head. "No."

When they reached the first floor, the man stooped to bring his face close to Angela's, squeezing her hand, his wife stroking her hair. "You don't have to see him at all, you know," he said. "You can just send him away."

The girl sniffled, rubbed the back of her hand under her nose, blew it loudly when the woman gave her a handkerchief, then dried her eyes with the corners of the cloth.

Of course, the girl was upset. Philip tried to imagine how this day had been for her, preparing to face a man who had abandoned her ten years ago, a man her mother despised, a man she didn't even know well enough to recognize. He was tempted to reveal his true identity, reach for his wallet, slide out a driver's license, hold the photo up to their faces. "That's me. I'm not like him at all. This is who I really am."

But before he could decide, Angela said, "No. It's all right. I'll go with him." She gestured toward Philip, suddenly defiant. "I'll get it over with."

"Let's go then." He moved to press a hand into her back, but froze, afraid to touch her, knowing that she and the couple saw the broken gesture.

The couple came out to the car with them, Philip leading the way to the curb, the woman lagging behind, buttoning Angela's jacket as they walked together, the man memorizing the license plate. "I want you back by ten," the woman stressed. "Your mother insists. Call us right away if there's any trouble. We'll come get you." She buckled Angela's seat belt, leaning inside the car, reluctant to give way, to let Philip move from the curb. "Are you absolutely sure?" the man asked. Angela nodded, kissed the woman's cheek and touched her lightly on the shoulder. Then the woman stepped back, and Philip drove off.

When they reached a stop sign several blocks away, Philip still hadn't spoken, knew it was up to him, certain the girl would not offer the first words. "You're looking fine," he made himself say.

"How would you know? I'm underweight. I'm skin and bones. I don't eat."

"Don't tell me you have one of those disorders?" Philip said, concerned, unsure how to react if she admitted she did.

"I just don't have an appetite. I've never had an appetite."

"What does your mother say?"

"What do you care what she says? You'd only tell me she was wrong, start shouting what an idiot she was, how everything she did or said or thought was ridiculous."

"Is that how you remember it?" He saw the girl was trembling, her voice shrill, at the edge of screaming.

"I still dream about it. How two people could hate each other so much."

"Does she still hate me?" He almost said "your father," wondering what would happen if he told her how much he loathed Arthur Weigant.

The girl pinched her face. "As much as you hate her."

Philip pictured his wife, felt an ache of longing that made him blink back tears. "Your parents' failings don't have to be yours," he said.

"You don't know anything about what it's like to be me." She made fists and pounded the dashboard, beating it like a child in a tantrum.

As much as he was tempted to shout at her to stop it, Philip forced a benign expression. "Is there anything I could do to make you like me? For us to start new?" He imagined himself entering the hotel with Angela at his side, smiling her affection, looking up at him with love, the two of them walking past Arthur Weigant as if he did not exist.

But the girl snarled her reply. "All I want is a finish. The absolute end of you."

"Then why did you come tonight?"

"I had to know what you looked like."

"And what do you see?"

"Someone awful. Rotten. Spiteful and mean."

"And what if other people thought I wasn't like that at all?"

"I'd say they were crazy." She dug her scuffed shoes at the floor mat, reached hands deep into the canvas purse on her lap.

For an instant, when her fingers clutched inside the purse, Philip half expected her to pull out a gun and point it at his face. Stop, he would cry; I'm a decent man. But her hands went limp.

He eased into the highway traffic, driving cautiously, even more than he did with his own children. He felt the terrible burden of this frail girl, the desperation of her need.

"I want you to forgive me."

"No. Never."

Just then Philip saw the turnoff sign for his town and felt an urge to take her home, confront her with his wife and children. He imagined pulling onto the ramp, telling Angela, I'm going to save you. For a moment he had a fantasy of her wanting to stay with them, with people who truly cared for one another. But he pictured the expressions of his wife and children if he brought this girl into their living room, and he knew he would never be able to explain the whim of this deception.

Philip drove on in silence, dazzled by the lights of the oncoming traffic. "This is the strangest night of my life," he told her.

"What about me?" she cried.

"I'm sure it's awful for you."

"Everything's always been awful. It always will be."

"Then forget you ever had a father." Philip spoke in his own voice, as himself.

Angela turned abruptly, for the first time stared into his face. But before he could meet her gaze, her eyes flowed tears; she collapsed in sobs, wrapping her arms around her middle and rocking back and forth. The pain of her look made him shudder.

Angela settled into a soft weeping, Philip driving on with no idea what to do next. Then a half mile ahead he saw the hotel with Arthur Weigant waiting inside, dark brick and glass, its lights dazzling far above the highway.

As they neared the hotel drive, he knew he should turn in, admit everything, deliver the girl to her real father. But his arms were rigid on the steering wheel, refusing to act on his thought. Then, seconds later, the hotel was gone, a shrinking reflection in the rearview mirror.

"I'll take you home now," he said.

"Yes." Her voice was so faint he wasn't sure she had spoken.

Philip knew they had nothing left to say to each other. They would ride in silence; Angela would get out, slam the door, never look back. She would hate Arthur Weigant forever, Philip's face the one haunting her dreams.

Philip would return to the hotel and tell the man his daughter refused to see him. For the rest of his life he would remember this night, reliving every word, every moment, a prisoner of his shame.

Brother

Every evening the first week after his brother Jim's funeral, Raymond called Sylvia, his sister-in-law, frustrated to be living 300 miles away. By the second week, Janie gave him one of her looks each time he reached for the phone. "Let them get through this themselves," she finally said. "I can't help it," he told his wife. "They're Jim's family. Mine too."

Usually one of his nieces answered, Vicki or Beth, both still in high school, nothing like their mother, with Jim's narrow frame and small features, echoes of each other, not really pretty but sweetfaced, appealing. Raymond did most of the talking, asking a dozen questions about school and their jobs, rarely referring to their father's death or even to his life. But when Raymond said something like "Your dad would be glad to know that," it was as if they hadn't heard.

All their lives he had been telling the girls he loved them like his own daughters, the children he and Janie longed for to tears in the first years of their marriage but never had. Arriving at the church before Jim's funeral, Raymond had rushed to them, wrapping an arm around each and pulling their faces against his chest. "Hey," he said, "my brother was a good man, and he had two fine girls. You both made him very happy. I'm proud you're my nieces."

The few times Sylvia answered his call, after a long ringing, he kept offering help, anything she needed, while she said nothing more than "I'm all right" or "Not now." He could picture her gripping the phone in clenched fingers, eager to hang up, face twisted at the sound of his voice.

"Are you blaming me for being alive?" he wanted to ask. Some night, he told himself, he would bring himself to do that, to find out what was so wrong.

●

Then, the forth week after the funeral, no one answered, even when he called back at bedtime, not Vicki or Beth or Sylvia. "They probably needed a change of scene," Janie offered. "Maybe they went to stay with her mother,"

"She doesn't like her mother," Raymond told her. "Jim always said so."

"Maybe that doesn't matter now."

"Maybe they're sitting there waiting for the ringing to stop. Maybe they're sick of my calling so much."

"Didn't I warn you?"

"He was my brother. He'd have wanted me to worry about them. I loved him."

●

He'd wanted to love his brother's wife too, but in the twenty-some years of her marriage to Jim she'd never let him. From the day they were born, he'd loved Vicki and Beth, and didn't care whether his nieces loved him back, though he believed they did. But he couldn't warm to Sylvia and felt guilty for his lack. Jim never complained about his wife. When he did talk about her, it was only reports of things she did, not about who she was.

At the funeral she had worn a black skirt, black jacket, black high heels, her hair curled and fluffed, the large round frames of her glasses glittering with golden specks. When Jim married her, she had been a drab young woman, dull hair hanging slack against her long face, her shoulders slumped as if she were trying to shrink and hide. Though he'd never told anyone, not even Janie, Raymond liked her better then, when she was bleak and skittish, folding into herself whenever he embraced her in a greeting. He thought maybe that was why Jim married her, a sense that she would evaporate if someone didn't take hold of her. Then between visits from one year to the next, she remade herself and became another person, acting as if she'd just learned she'd been cheated out of a million dollars.

"He did the best he could," Raymond told her when they stood together beside the casket.

"And what good was that?"

•

Jim died at an inconvenient time for Raymond — when he had to be on the road all day getting ready for the holiday season, covering every store on his route, up till midnight processing orders for items people gave as gifts and never used themselves. "What a hell of a way to make a living," he'd always say to Jim. The sudden ringing of Sylvia's call had startled him; his fingers splayed across the calculator, spewing out a jumble of numbers on a tape that, later, he folded in his wallet and saved as if it were a record of his brother's death.

Raymond had picked up the phone at once to stifle the sound, then cleared his throat and waited for the buzz of the calculator to stop. But, before he could speak, Sylvia said, "He's dead."

"When?" There was no need to ask how or why.

"This morning."

"Why didn't you call right away?"

"I couldn't find your number. Things were busy here. He was lying in the middle of the kitchen floor."

Her voice was so flat, so empty that Raymond worried she was in shock. "And how are you doing?"

"I'm me. I'm always me."

"Your daughters?"

"You'll have to ask them."

"Do you want me to come? If I leave now, I can be there before dawn."

"I don't want anything," Sylvia had told him. "There's a funeral. You can come for that." She gave him date, time, place, then hung up before he could tell her how sorry he was.

"Goddamn you!" Raymond had slammed the phone, smacked

fists on the table, scattering order forms across the carpet.

•

Of course, Jim shouldn't have died at all. A man just past fifty should have lived on for years, not tumbled from a kitchen chair in the middle of breakfast with a burst aorta. But Raymond had been warning him for years, the way you warn someone when you barely believe what you're saying is real: "You've had two bypass operations. Slow down. Exercise. Lose that gut." And Jim would tell him "Sure, sure. No more greasy ribs. Just one order of fries. I'll buy a bike." Then his eyes would crinkle in the same smile that had been disarming Raymond since they were children, turning exasperation into laughter.

After the funeral, Raymond sat for hours in the evenings looking through a box of old photographs, loose pictures he'd always been meaning to paste down in a album — the two of them on tricycles, in scout uniforms, leaning against their first cars, posed with fishing rods, smirking in high school caps and gowns, standing stiffly between their long-dead parents. A factory accident, exploding chemicals, had killed their father when both sons were both in the army, stationed at opposite sides of the world, Jim arriving too late for a transfer on a cargo plane in Guam and missing the burial. Their mother died six months after Jim's wedding, wasted from a cancer that had been eating at her for years.

Most people didn't take them for bothers, Raymond so much bigger and darker, Jim fair and wiry despite his appetite until his middle bloated when he hit his forties, as if every meal he'd ever eaten suddenly accumulated in his gut.

Raymond spread the photos on a tabletop arranged by age, a panorama of his brother's life, his too, right beside him. He stared at their images until his eyes stung with tears.

•

Though he worried constantly about their failure to answer, Raymond waited a few days before calling Sylvia and the girls again,

159

listening to Janie and letting a weekend go by, intending to delay even longer but unable to keep himself from dialing on Monday night. This time the ringing was strange; he heard a clicking and a computer voice telling him Jim's phone was no longer connected. He dailed again, very carefully this time, and received the same message. Then he got a live operator for verification. "It's impossible!" he cried. "I'm sorry, sir," was all she would say.

Janie found the number for Sylvia's mother in a pile of old letters. She lived in the mountains several hours west of Jim and Sylvia's town. "I don't know anything about her," the woman told Raymond.

"You must," he insisted.

"My daughter don't talk to me. I had to hear about her husband from strangers."

"What do you think could be wrong?"

"You'll have to ask her."

"I don't know where she is."

"Then find her."

·

Raymond threw clean underwear, a razor, and his toothbrush in an overnight bag. If he left now, he could be there before dawn. Janie offered to come along, but he knew she was just humoring him. He told her there was no sense in two of them rushing off in the middle of the night, and — besides — she had to go to work. "So do you," she said. He gave her a stricken look. "I can't until I know something."

On the interstate, Raymond held the car at 80, roaring into the darkness, driving the way he had the morning of Jim's funeral, Janie beside him then, tense, shouting at him that he would kill them both. "You'll have your own funeral, mine too!" When he slowed down, she began to cry. Now, a month later, alone, he cried himself.

The night Jim died he and Janie had sat in the living room, every light on full, barely remembering to sip from cups of tepid coffee, she wiping her eyes with a napkin.

"I haven't talked to Jim in weeks," he had said. "I let myself get so busy that I didn't take time to call. We haven't seen him in over a year. Jesus, we'll never see him again."

"He didn't call you either," she had told him. "It doesn't mean anything. People forget to do things. He always knew how you cared about him."

"All my life, I've had a brother. And now I don't."

Raymond realized he was clenching the steering wheel, grinding his teeth. He ached all over, a big man, a head taller than Jim had been, not fat but thickly built, his trunk too heavy for his legs, joints giving him pain most of the time now. He spoke out loud: "I don't know where I'm going."

•

He reached Jim's house at dawn, mist thick on his windshield, the sunglow barely streaking through grey clouds. The house was small, the home of a man who just got by, a one-storey, two-bedroom clapboard overwhelmed by dense shrubs on an acre of weeds that Jim rarely bothered to mow, Janie's eyes red with allergies the whole time during their visits. But as Raymond liked to say, amused at the thought, "There's lots of things Jim doesn't bother to do. You're lucky you never had to share a room with him."

His car pitched over the ruts of the dirt drive, bottoming out on the springs. Even before he reached the house, he heard the dogs, howling as if in great pain. After the burial, when the people from the church left and the house became quiet, Raymond realized Jim's dogs had been yelping the whole time, the three of them tied to a shed next to an outbuilding where Jim had stored his tools. Janie and the girls didn't seem to notice, but the sound unnerved him so much he looked for Sylvia to shut them up. Beth told him she had gone to her room. He knocked on the door, then opened it when she didn't answer. She was standing at a mirror staring at herself, not even glancing at his reflection when he entered.

"What are you going to do with Jim's dogs?" he said.

"Shoot them."

"I'm serious."

"So am I."

Now when Raymond hurried from the car, they hurled themselves at their chains, snarling at him, fierce in their fury. He realized they hadn't been fed for days and retrieved a bag of food from the shed, tearing it open and throwing it down on the hard ground. The dogs buried their snouts in the pellets, bodies quivering as they gulped.

He expected to have to break into the house, but the door opened when he turned the knob. The living room looked just as he remembered it, the same furniture Jim and Sylvia had owned through their marriage, cheap and sagging, but spotless, Sylvia's obsession, always harping at Jim to pick up after himself. The kitchen gleamed as he stood in the doorway, polished pots hanging from a pegboard, dishes stacked on the shelves, boxes and cans aligned in the cabinets. The refrigerator dazzled him with a bare white glare.

He stepped into the girls' bedroom first, struck by its neatness, a row of stuffed animals on a bookcase, drawers shut tight, spreads tucked in under the pillows. The closet was empty, just wire hangers tangled on a bar, and the dresser too, except for one wadded garment that made him imagine a rushed packing.

In Sylvia's room, the one she had shared with Jim, the shades were down, everything blurred in a grey haze. The dresser tops were clear, the bed stripped, sheets carefully folded atop the blanket at the foot of the mattress. Only the closet door was wide open, not a garment inside, but two cardboard boxes stacked on the floor. Even before Raymond opened them, he knew Jim's clothes were inside — shirts, trousers, jackets, shoes, his one good suit, three ties draped across the top.

Though he knew he was wasting time, Raymond unpacked the boxes, smoothing the clothes on hangers, buttoning the shirt fronts, matching the shoes and placing them in one long row. Then he made the bed, squaring the corners the way he had once learned in the army.

When he was finished, he went to the kitchen, forcing himself to step inside, backing against a wall, studying the linoleum for the place Jim had sprawled in the instant of his death, remembering movies where white chalk outlined the spot where the body had lain. Then, taking care not to step in the center of the room, he sat in a chair, the same one he always seemed to pick on his visits to his brother, the rungs popping loose no matter how many times Sylvia had badgered Jim into gluing them.

•

He and Jim would talk for hours in that kitchen, up long past midnight, a coffee pot bubbling on the stove; but now it struck Raymond that they never really said anything. Their conversations were always about their jobs, tuning up cars, the cost of things, now and then memories of boyhood foolishness, the time a wheel came loose off Jim's old Ford and rolled past them on the highway. They'd roar laughing every time they told each other that story, Jim stamping his feet on the floor, Raymond burying his head in his arms on the tabletop and shaking in his chair.

But they never spoke of how they felt about being brothers or living their lives. How Jim felt about being a father or Raymond about being childless. About the women they married. About who and what they loved.

When Jim started complaining about his boss, Raymond would look at his watch. Jim worked for the county, usually on road crews, plowing snow in winter, patching tar and trimming trees in summer, with enough seniority to stay inside the pickup trucks while others hauled and lifted. His boss had been a pain in the ass for a dozen years, and it had gotten so that Raymond could repeat Jim's gripes from memory. Jim would catch him glancing at his watch and grin. "Let's go rescue our wives," he'd say. The two women had been sitting in the living room the whole time, and Raymond never could bring himself to ask, "From what?"

•

There're weren't many neighbors near Jim's house, the closest across the road in a yard filled with old cars and delivery vans, stripped engines swinging from block and tackle under two tarpaulins. Rayond shouted, "Hello," and then rapped on the screen door. He could smell cabbage cooking at the back of the house. Though he was hungry, he didn't have any appetite. After he rapped and called again, a young woman came out onto the porch, a skinny thing with dark sunken eyes.

She just stared at him when he introduced himself. She didn't know Sylvia and the girls well. All they'd done was nod and wave when they saw each other. Yes, she'd seen the car drive away a week or so ago. It looked like a lot of stuff was piled on the back seat. But she wasn't the kind to ask questions about other people's business.

The minister who had buried Jim was friendlier in a professional sort of way, his voice rich and heartfelt, full of sympathy for the family. But he knew no more than the neighbor. When he'd tried to counsel Sylvia, she seemed impatient with his visits. Vicki and Beth were polite but did no more than nod when he spoke to them and kept glancing at their mother. He'd asked about her plans, and she told him she had none. His guess was that she'd run off on a sudden impulse, panic at being a widow, would probably come back because everything she owned was in that house, though Raymond was sure she wanted none of it.

The deputy sheriff Raymond spoke with knew Jim well from his county work. They'd had a few beers together, even planned fishing trips, though none of them had ever happened. "Your brother was the kind of guy everybody liked."

"What about his wife?"

"She sort of kept to herself."

And she had a right to go wherever she had gone, Raymond realized. There was no law that you had to tell anybody, even family, what you were up to.

•

"If she wanted to run away so bad, why did she wait so long? Why didn't she do it when Jim was alive?" he asked Janie back home. "Nothing makes any sense."

"Who says it's supposed to?"

It was the kind of thing she said when she was joking, but right now Raymond couldn't tell. Her lips were tight, eyes staring down at the rug. He'd woken her up slamming the door when he came in.

"You mad at me?" he asked. His joints ached. He'd been driving for hours, the car fan still whirring in the driveway,

Janie hunched in her bathrobe, bare feet tucked under her on the sofa. "Do you know how late it is?"

"That's not an answer."

"I don't bother being angry with you any more. Not in years. It doesn't do any good."

"What did you talk about with Sylvia?"

"When?"

"All those visits, when I was with Jim in the kitchen?"

"She didn't have much to say. Most of the time we watched TV."

"She must have told you something." Raymond sensed that she was holding back.

"Now and then. It was a lot of years."

"Why didn't she like me?"

She gave him an expression of bewilderment. "Couldn't you tell? The way she cringed any time you walked through a door."

Raymond went rigid, as if she had slapped his face. "What did I ever do to her?"

Janie rubbed her ankle, hard, like someone kneading a pain. "Maybe it was the size of you. You so big and their rooms so small. You overwhelmed the place, laughing and hugging everybody, lifting their feet off the ground, talking a mile a minute. Like you were sucking up all the oxygen."

"For God's sake, it was my brother's house!"

"You were in their lives too much. You tried too hard."

"Did she tell you that?"

"It's what I saw."

"What about Jim? Did he see it too?"

Janie hunched over and pulled her arms tight, shivering though the night was warm. "You were brothers. You were used to each other."

"Maybe he cringed too. Maybe he didn't want me there either."

"What he didn't want was you in the same room as Sylvia. I could almost hear his brain racing to come up with ways to get you off somewhere else."

Raymond paced a circle and braced his hands against the wall, as if it would cave in if he let go. "I always felt so sorry for Jim. Having to live every day of his life with a woman like that. I could never imagine him being happy."

"There's no telling what makes people happy. Or unhappy."

He turned and moved across to the sofa, standing above her, hands rigid at his side. "And what about you? Are you happy?"

Janie met his eyes, and he couldn't breathe, felt his chest heaving through her silence. "Our lives are together," she finally said. "These are the only lives we'll ever have. This is who we are, all we'll ever be."

"What if you decide to take off some day?"

"Where would I go?" Janie shrugged but did not smile.

The flesh of her face was loosening; maybe it had been for years, but now in the shadow of one dim table lamp she looked so much older. Of course, they'd been married for almost thirty years. Someday she would die and he would die, one of them first, leaving the other alone. That wouldn't be for a while. Unlike Jim, he took care of himself. He'd be selling people useless knickknacks till he was a very old man.

"Do you think we'll ever find them?" he asked her.

"Would it make any difference if we did?"

Raymond shook his head. For the first time he wanted to curse his brother for dying.

Islands

Fire Island

They walked most of the way to Ocean Beach on the packed wet sand at the water's edge, Mike holding Lucy's hand as the last foam of breakers curled around their ankles. Lucy laughed and skipped, settling on her toes like a dancer. Mike watched her feet, watched his own as they splashed impressions in the sand. He was nineteen and barefoot beneath the sun.

Mike slipped his hand from Lucy's and sprinted across the beach to the dunes, toppling backwards with outstretched arms and legs. Lucy ran after and threw herself beside him. He wrapped his arms around her and squeezed as hard as he could. She cried "Oomph!" and kissed his neck.

Then they just lay looking up at the deep blue sky, together watching the wisps of clouds poised far above them, listened to the rush of the sea, saw the gulls gliding in wide circles. He pressed his foot against hers, touched fingertips along her tanned arm.

"I never want to go back," Lucy said. "It's perfect here."

"Yes." The word caught in his throat and tears flooded his eyes. He could not express his emotion, reveal how much he had longed for this moment in this place. He kissed her lightly because he did not trust himself to kiss her hard even though the beach around them was empty.

Lucy hopped to her feet, playful again, gripped his wrist and pulled him up. "Come on. We can't lie here all day and forget what we came for."

"Booze!" He gave a cheerleader's yell.

Lucy began chanting, "Booze, booze, booze," and he chanted along with her, the two of them marching lockstep over the dunes, up onto the paths by the cottages, until they reached the sidewalk of the village.

The liquor store clerk, a student himself, crewcut and deeply tanned, wearing penny loafers and summer weight flannels that Mike admired, sold them a fifth of Canadian Club without asking for proof of age. They exchanged broad smiles of complicity as if they were people free from rules.

By the time Mike and Lucy walked the three miles back to the inn, the sun was setting brilliantly. He had never before paid attention to the beauty of sunsets. "Look," he cried and stepped back to see Lucy shimmering in a pink glow. "Look!" She reached out and squeezed his hand.

In his room Mike measured Canadian Club by eye into a tennis ball can, added ice, sugar, and lemon juice to shake up a batch of whisky sours. They drank from paper cups, touching the rims in celebration of being tanned and barefoot and together.

At nightfall, in deepening shadows, they undressed, quickly removing their few garments — shorts, tee shirts, underpants. When they stood naked, they gazed at each other, Mike at the untanned stripes around her breasts and loins, at her tiny nipples, the pubic patch. Lucy was a small girl, short but solid in an athletic way, her hair in tight curls, her nose dotted with freckles. As he enfolded her into his arms, he was sure he would love her forever.

Manhattan

Adrianne sprawled face down on the chaise lounge while Mike rubbed lotion into her back. He traced a double dose along the pink grooves etched by her now unsnapped bathing suit top, stole fingertips to press the soft white breasts. A thousand windows peered down from the apartment houses that rose above the three spindly trees of the yard, but Mike blanked them out of his awareness, pretended they were surrounded by nothing but sheer rock face.

He had been lucky to find a garden in the city, four steps up from his basement efficiency and shared with the tenants on the first floor of the brownstone, a forty-year-old bachelor named Teddy Keane and a hostile German shepherd named Tiger. Adrianne called the garden a treasure. She loved it.

It was a warm Sunday, sections of the *Times* scattered across the slate patio, the dog safely chained to a wrought iron railing. Although the time was past noon Teddy had not stirred. They had the garden to themselves.

Mike rubbed hard into the small of her back. Adrianne placed a hand on his thigh. "Oh, that's nice." Her engagement ring flashed in the sun, impressive, Mike once again satisfied with his choices — the ring and the girl. She had stayed all last night, sleeping beside him for the third time since their engagement, more relaxed each time, accepting the naturalness of the occasion but still shy with her sexuality.

She was so sweet and sensitive, so soft. It pleased Mike to comfort her with his embrace, wipe away tears of insecurity with a fingertip. Although firm-fleshed, she seemed fragile, afraid to make decisions, depending upon him for all important choices, stunning him during his first serious attempt at seduction by asking him what she should do.

Adrianne sighed, her flesh yielding to the pressure of his fingertips, and Mike had a vision of his future with this young woman: no matter what he wanted, what he did, she would submit. When his hand brushed her cheek, Adrianne seized it and kissed his palm.

"We're invading your pleasure garden." Teddy called down to them from the back door of his apartment. Tiger barked and leaped at the end of his chain. Adrianne quickly fastened her suit top and sat up. "Who's we?" Mike asked as he capped the bottle of lotion.

"Teddy and friends."

Teddy opened the screen for two men and two women, made introductions, and immediately organized everyone into setting up folding tables to spread lox, bagels, cream cheese, and the makings for bloody marys. The two men were Teddy's age, both in seersucker jackets and tennis sneakers. One of the women, white haired and young faced, made herself very busy as server, rattling wrists jammed with bracelets. Only one of their names stuck with Mike, Susan, a girl no older than himself, only a few inches shorter, lovely and slender, immaculate in a gauzy dress on this glowing summer's day.

Tiger roamed free now, fetching a plastic bone each time Teddy tossed it, indifferent to the others. The dog became a subject of conversation, then the garden, the day, the joy of such a Sunday in the city.

When Adrianne went inside to change from her bathing suit, embarrassed to be so scantily dressed, Mike spoke alone with Susan in a corner of the garden. He gestured toward Teddy and the others. "I haven't gotten you all straight yet. Who's with you?"

"I'm with myself," she said.

"Is that a general condition?"

"As long as I choose."

By the time Adrianne returned he had asked Susan for her address. Whenever their eyes met through the rest of the afternoon, she smiled as if sharing a secret.

Mallorca

A path wound down through the olive groves from their cottage to the Mediterranean. The nights were cool; they slept under his down sleeping bag unzipped into a quilt. But the bright morning sun brought quick warmth. Each day Mike and Susan dressed directly into their bathing suits and carried a straw bag of bread, almond paste, and oranges to the rocks at the blue water's edge for their breakfast. The billy goat fettered beside the path clanked his bell and ignored them, the chickens ran fluttering form their steps. It was the same every morning: goat, chickens, bread, almond paste, oranges, and bright sun.

Before eating they lay on their backs on a rock twenty feet above the sea and let the sun penetrate them. The rock itself was hollow with a small opening in the surface near the spot where they rested their heads. Each splash of waves forced a whoosh of air through the hole, a sound like the murmur of a human voice. Mike and Susan called it the Whispering Rock and kept it a secret from their friends, the one thing on this island that belonged to them alone.

Mike was hungry. He hand touched the straw bag, but he did not want to sit up yet. He shielded his eyes with a forearm and watched Susan, her belly showing the first bulge of pregnancy above the bikini bottom.

He was sure he wanted a child; they had discussed the consequences endlessly during the first four years of marriage. But he regretted her pregnancy as if it were about to spoil something vital in her. Perhaps it was because he had admired her slender body so much, the absolute flatness of her stomach.

Susan sensed him looking and flipped back the brim of her sun hat. "What are you thinking?"

"Nothing," he said. "Just enjoying being here."

"I'm starting to show, aren't I?"

"A little."

"And you don't like it."

"I want this baby as much as you do."

"But you're scared."

"Of what?"

"The changes in me. The threat to your sex life. The uncertainty of knowing that in the future there'll never be just the two of us again."

Mike shrugged and turned to face the sea, the dazzling ripple of reflected sun. It upset him that she always had to analyze and define. Even about the Whispering Rock she explained point by point why the secret was so important to their relationship. He let the dazzle stun his vision.

"You're annoyed with me, aren't you?" Susan said.

"I'm hungry." Mike blinked, sat up, and passed the bag to her.

She spread almond paste on two pieces of bread and handed him one. He nodded thanks and chewed it in two bites. After the bread they peeled oranges and spat the pits down to the sea. On an impulse Mike leaned forward to lick the juice that ran down her chin. She laughed and drew away as if his gesture had been a tease. Just then he heard chicken squawks and the crunch of footsteps on the path behind them.

It was Mary Chin, the Chinese girl. That's what Mike and Susan called her even though she had been born in Rapid City, South Dakota, and spoke with a Midwestern twang. The one time they invited Mary for dinner she drank half a bottle of cognac and fell asleep on the sofa bed. Mike had to walk her home with a flashlight through the darkness, wrapping an arm around her shoulder to hold her steady. At the door of her house she collapsed against him with a long melting kiss. Mike responded, thinking all the time that she would not remember this in the morning.

He offered her bread despite the frown in Susan's eyes.

"I've seen you here before," Mary said. "It looked so pleasant I couldn't resist coming down. Do you mind?"

"Of course not," he said.

Mary stretched out to the left of Mike. She wore white shorts and a tank top. Her skin was bronzed from hours in the sun.

"What's that sound?" she asked.

"The rock," Mike said. "It talks."

"What does it say?"

"Whatever you want to hear."

The three of them lay there for half an hour, Susan deliberately silent Mike could tell, Mary chattering away about last night's party at Rafael's.

Finally Susan spoke. "I'm going back up to the cottage."

She stood long-legged in the bikini knotted on her hip bones. The slight bowing at her knees excited Mike, but he debated staying behind with Mary. He decided he had better stand beside his wife. Mary said she would go up too. She followed Susan on the path with Mike last. To his surprise in the thick of the olive trees Mary reached a hand behind her to squeeze his. He squeezed back as chickens fled and the goat clanked his bell.

MARTHA'S VINEYARD

Mike hadn't been on a bicycle for years, but renting one seemed de rigueur in Edgartown, the best way to explore the narrow streets lined with white houses each once owned by a whaling captain. Or so it

172

seemed. They rented from a stand near the town's pier amid restaurants, fast seafood stalls, ice cream parlors, and gift shops, an area thick with tourists in madras and sandals.

It took Mike a few moments to get his balance and maneuver around the clusters of people. Susan adjusted at once, erect and striking on her seat, shifting through the gears as if it were something she had done every day of her life.

Mike lost sight of her at South Water Street. She was moving swiftly and easily. Cyclists had to obey the one-way signs, so he could not take a short cut in the direction he thought she had gone. He rode up and back on South Water, then turned onto Main and saw her ahead pausing to skim the menu outside a crepérie. But by the time he reached the place she was gone. Five minutes later she waved to him at a residential corner and sprinted away.

"I'm not racing," he called even though she could not hear. "I quit."

He wheeled around in the direction opposite hers and moved down back streets without caring about scenery, trying not to think, knowing that when he stopped he would have to make a decision.

He ended up at the far end of North Water Street in front of a large hotel of darkly weathered shingles. He crossed over to the beach and pushed the bicycle along the plank walkway to the lighthouse. Only a few people were on the sand, a fat old woman in a black swimsuit that seemed to come in layers, a lone young man fully dressed on a towel, three teenage girls flaunting ripe tanned bodies. Most of the bathers in Edgartown chose to ferry to Chappaquiddick. Across the water from where he stood, beyond gliding sailboats, Mike could see the bright beach tents, children splashing in the surf, dozens of people sprawled beneath the glowing sun. The brilliance made his eyes ache, and it struck him how far all these people were from his life.

They would be divorced. At least he accepted the certainly of it, glad the boys were hundreds of miles away at summer camp where their nearness could not confuse his emotions. When he found Susan at the inn, he would speak calmly, sure of her agreement. Then, perhaps, they could enjoy their vacation.

Mykonos

"I envy you all the places you've been," Dolores said. "All my life I've dreamed of travel but never go anywhere."

"That's because you chose to have so many children," Mike said. "You can't build a nest and indulge wanderlust at the same time."

"But I want to do everything."

They sat at a corner table where the light was so dim he felt a grey film covered his eyes. Except for a few men on stools in the other room, the bar was empty. It always was on Monday nights when they met there, arriving in separate cars. Mike held Dolores's hand in both of his on the tabletop, pleased with his urge to lean across and kiss her.

"If you could pick any place in the world," he asked her, "where would you go first?"

"Mykonos."

"What's that?"

"An island in the Aegean."

"Why?"

"It's so beautiful in pictures. I can't imagine how a place could be more beautiful. When life gets awful — through all the trouble with Tom — I bring out my pictures of Mykonos and keep my sanity."

"What's it like?"

"White houses on cliffs rising from the sea. A sky the bluest of blues. It's perfect. I dream that if I could go there everything would be all right."

This woman of forty, greying, skin puckering about her pale eyes, was more innocent than her three adolescent daughters. Mike tried to picture her standing on a cliff against the blue sky of Mykonos, youthful and radiant.

"I'll take you," he said.

She laughed, her face suddenly flushed. "Don't tease."

"It would be a bit of a rush to arrange things. But we can leave within the month."

Tears welled when she realized he was serious. She pressed his hands. He thought she might weep. "Oh, Mike, I couldn't."

"Why not?"

She met his eyes, wavered, and then looked down. "I can't." Her denial was almost a sob.

"Are you afraid Mykonos will disappoint you?"

"No. It's just not possible." Now her tears flowed.

As they clutched each other's hands in the darkness, Mike knew they would never go to Mykonos together.

OCRACOKE

"Where are all the goddamned ponies?" Lorraine said.

They had parked across the highway by the ocean and now stood on a wooden platform overlooking a strip of fenced off land on the sound side of the island.

"The sign promised wild ponies," she insisted.

"There." Mike pointed to a cluster several hundred yards away across grey sand and stiff beach grass.

"One, two, three . . . six." She counted with a finger. "You said hundreds."

He looked at Lorraine and shrugged. She was the kind of woman who had never appealed to him — too hefty, too loud, blonde hair puffed and brittle with spray; the bathroom of her apartment littered with dye packs, curling iron, rollers, spray cans; her conversation underlined with sarcasms. And yet they had taken this vacation together. And for months of Saturday nights they had crawled bleary-eyed into her unmade bed to clutch at each other's flesh.

"George Hoffman told me there were hundreds of wild ponies here," he said.

"That was how long ago?"

"About twenty-five years. We worked together when I had my first job."

"Times change, Michael. You've never caught on."

"He'd talk about Ocracoke by the hour, made it seem like another world."

"Fifteen miles of sand and scrub grass. Terrific."

"The ponies descend from some of the first Spanish horses to be brought to America. They're absolutely pure bred."

"I count six, Michael. Six lousy horses."

"Since that time I've always wanted to come to Ocracoke."

"Congratulations. You've finally made it. Glorious Ocracoke."

"I guess we might as well turn back."

"My thoughts exactly."

Lorraine's highheeled sandals wobbled on the sand path to the car. Mike lagged behind, then stopped to watch her pull away from him as if unaware that he was following. But when she kicked off her shoes and stood poised on a dune, silhouetted against the glowing orange sun, he ran ahead to fling an arm around her waist.

Hiding Place

The words came out in a nasal whimper — "Please visit your mother" — a mournful pleading, but Gregory knew it was a command. His grandmother's eyes overflowed tears, her throat quivering as if she would break into a deep sobbing. He couldn't remember a time when this a small, plump woman with a witch's beaked nose hadn't frightened him, as much as she caressed him and called him Honey, Sweetie. Even as a toddler he knew it would be much worse for him if he stiffened, if he fought her embraces. Now at ten he let her pull him into her loose flesh, lock him against her with thick arms. He had no choice. His father — sitting across the room on a straight wooden chair, folded into himself, staring down at his knotted hands — wouldn't save him. He would have to visit his mother.

He knew his father would not be with him. The man lived in silence now, speaking only to ask if he had eaten, if he needed clean clothes. Flat, drained. When Gregory, young as he was, looked at his father, he understood absolute helplessness. But he remembered his father ranting at his mother, the man's voice resounding with rage: "You don't have enemies! Nobody wants to hurt us! You're imagining everything!" And his mother backed against a wall, emaciated, unwashed, hair in dark knots, tapping a cigarette against her lips — first upper, then lower, again and again, an endless ritual. She stood rigid as if not hearing a word, as if she were somewhere else, until a growl ripped from her throat; "Don't believe him! He's a liar! He's always been a liar!" One of her voices — Dr. Trapp. His father would beat the air. And Gregory, standing at the top of the stairway, watching from the shadows, wanted to cry down to them, Shut up! shut up! But he said nothing, just waited until his father turned and left the room, his mother gazing out with a faint smile, oblivious to the inch-long ash that dropped onto the carpet.

Gregory could recognize most of the voices. His mother's had been soft once, but now she rarely spoke for herself. The harsh one, Dr. Trapp, dominated, cursing, demanding, rebuking. There was the hissing Betty Jean, the whispering Byron, the giggling Sixty-Eight, the stammering Uncle Duty; voices that claimed to be his grandmother and his father, but never him, no voice that identified itself as Gregory.

Most nights, he would hear his bedroom door open and his mother shuffle in through the darkness, the only light the red glow of her cigarette as she stood over his bed intoning urgent voices. But they were subdued, even Dr. Trapp, as if part of her did not want to wake him. He held himself absolutely still, pretending to sleep, trying to decipher what they said, seeking clues that would explain what was happening to his mother, to his life. Every now and then he heard a voice say "the boy," yet the rest was blurred, none of it making any sense. Then once, in sounds that were truly her, his memory of her gentleness: "There's no place to hide, no place that's safe."

He wished for a lock on his door, once even went up to his father and asked, "Can I have . . . ," stopping abruptly when he saw the expression on the man's face. "What?" "Nothing." Gregory turned away, then went upstairs to tie a string between the doorknob and his bedpost, knotting it again and again, pulling it taut. That night when the door cracked he could hear her pushing against the string, three times, then four, and finally turning away, the voices getting louder, Dr. Trapp furious. Gregory sobbed, clutching the pillow as his body shuddered, the most he had ever cried for his mother. In the morning he unknotted the string and threw it deep into his closet.

When his grandmother visited, he stayed out in the yard pretending to play. But even there he could hear the shouts, his grandmother's hysterical "Why? Why? Why?" as if bewildered that her domination couldn't force a cure. From his mother, Dr. Trapp snarled, "Leave her alone, you bitch. You interfering bitch!" Once when he heard a crashing, Gregory rushed up to the window to see his mother seizing dishes from the cabinets and hurling them to the floor, his grandmother cowering in a doorway, hands fluttering wildly. In the evening his silent father swept up the debris with loud clatters.   After that they used plastic plates for the meals his father prepared, he and his father, his mother sitting with them but eating nothing, just drinking coffee and smoking, staring straight ahead, her mouth in a constant muttering.

At school Gregory's friends kept apart from him, as if he were contaminated. He missed their company but felt relief at not being asked questions, not having to explain. Each day, when school ended, he stayed away from his house till nightfall, walking the paths of a park where no one went, seeking unfamiliar streets, watching the play of children he did not know, hoping they would ask him to join, but turning away if one approached.

He wished he could talk to his father, daydreamed for hours about going up to him and saying, "Mommy's crazy, isn't she?" Then things might be different for him, for the two of them. But, because his father buried the fact of her madness in some dark place deep within, Gregory was afraid to speak.

When the ambulance came for his mother, he was shocked. Walking home from the school ground where he had stayed by himself till dusk, sitting on the seat of a swing, barely moving, dangling, he saw the neighbors gathered in their doorways, peeking out windows, his mother on the front porch screaming, flailing arms and legs, her hair wild, as she tried to rip away from the attendants, large men and women who wrestled her arms to her sides, tied them down and strapped her to a stretcher. When they slid her inside the ambulance, she let out a wail that pierced his brain.

By the time Gregory ran up the sidewalk to his house, his father was climbing into his car to follow the ambulance, his face ashen, the keys in his hand trembling. "Get inside," his father ordered. "Now!"

It was so quiet in the house, stiller than he had ever remembered it. Just the sound of his footsteps made him uneasy. He walked from room to room as if discovering a strange place. In the den, his father's sheets and blankets were piled in a corner, neatly folded, a pillow on top. In the bedroom his parents had once shared, the bed had only a bare mattress blotted with dark stains, scarred with cigarette burns.

The dresser drawers gaped open, the closet bare except for a tangle of hangers. All the clothing lay heaped in the middle of the carpet, a great tangled pile. Gregory closed the door, sorry he had opened it, unwilling to enter another room. He climbed into his bed, still dressed, but with the covers up to his face. When he heard his father returning home, he closed his eyes.

With his mother gone, his grandmother came almost every day, bringing meals that she had prepared in her kitchen, heavy food that Gregory had to eat with her sitting at the table, watching closely. She and his father would go into the den, the door closed, and he could hear only her voice speaking of doctors and drugs and therapy, persistent, demanding. Perhaps his father nodded; perhaps he just sat there.

And now three weeks after they took his mother away and Gregory could finally sleep, his grandmother was insisting that he visit her. "Your mother misses you. She asks for you all the time."

"When?" he said, fearing that she would take the question as defiance, that she would slap him, though she never had.

"Tonight," his grandmother smiled her triumph. "Visiting hours."

She drove, stubby hands on the steering wheel of the large black car that had been his grandfather's, Gregory on the front seat beside her, belted in, a strap tight across his chest. The car crept on back streets, making frequent turns, as if there were no direct route to where they had taken his mother. It was late November, the tall trees bare, dark branches outlined in the moonlight, leaves crunching under the tires. She leaned forward, peering through the windshield, the skin taut over her warped nose. He hoped she would get lost, never find the place, give up in cold silence and take him home.

But she began talking. "You may see a lot of strange people there. Don't pay attention to them. Just think how the doctors are helping your mother. How she'll be back with you soon. You'll be a family again."

Gregory didn't believe her, sensed that she was lying to herself more than to him. He tried to imagine what the strange people would be like, picturing a room filled with his mother's voices — Dr. Trapp, Sixty-Eight, Betty Jean, Byron, Uncle Duty. Would Betty Jean look like the woman who had been their neighbor, an abrupt woman with short dark hair and leathery skin who never said hello? His mother had brooded over the woman's attitude, talking about it endlessly when his father came home: "Why does she hate me so much? What did I do to her?" "Nothing," his father would say. "It's her, not you." But eventually his mother began claiming that Betty Jean wanted to hurt them all, give them pain, burn their house down. She stayed up all night, pacing from window to window, watching for movements in the shadows. His father sold the house, bought another, and still his mother became crazier, overwhelmed by voices.

"We're here." His grandmother startled him as she turned into a long drive marked by two thick stone columns. The great grey shape of a building loomed ahead, dim lights in small barred windows, a dark tower over the center entrance. It all seemed huge, overwhelming. Turn back! he wanted to cry. Turn back!

His grandmother parked in an arc of spaces at the front of the building, first at an odd angle, then backing up and pulling forward until she was satisfied. "I don't know why they make it so hard," she said, angry. "Come on. Get out."

She walked to his side, opening his door, taking his hand as if to guide him, but grasping, her palm hot and damp. A gravel path led to the building, sharp stones he could feel through the soles of his shoes. Though she was only a few inches taller than he, she pulled Gregory toward the front steps with a fierce determination. He noticed people outside, each one standing alone, barely moving, heads bent, their faces fogged by cigarette smoke. He would not look at them, did not want to see them.

Inside, his grandmother gripped his shoulders to guide him toward a counter. The space around them was a circular rotunda, the floor marble, the walls soaring upward to a skylight far above, designs molded into the plaster. Gregory realized that he had expected cells, rows of them like the prisons he had seen in movies, bare walls, bright lights, and shining steel bars, people strapped down, the way his mother had been on the stretcher.

From behind the counter a heavy, dark woman, her flesh bulging in a blue uniform, nodded to his grandmother and slid a lined pad toward her. He watched his grandmother sign her name and his mother's, the letters large circular loops that sprawled on the paper. "I know the way," she told the woman, defiant, as if the woman had insulted her, and pulled Gregory by the wrist.

They walked down a long corridor, turned a corner and followed another corridor. People were slipping in and out of doorways. Even though they wore street clothes, Gregory knew they were patients because the clothes did not match, did not fit, shirts inside out, buttoned askew, pants drooping, shoes untied, laces dragging on the floor tiles. All were smoking, cigarettes cupped in their hands as if they feared someone would steal them. They looked unwashed, hair tangled, smelling of urine. Most did not notice Gregory and his grandmother, but a few women smiled at him with broken yellow teeth, making small coaxing movements with their fingers. He edged closer to his grandmother, but she stepped ahead, tugging at his arm.

Then she stopped at a door with a frosted pane. He could see wire woven into the glass. She pulled it open and led him into a room with a jumble of plastic chairs and wooden tables, magazines and board games spilling onto the floor. But no one was playing, no one reading. Gregory coughed at the thick smoke. Several women stood backed against the walls; others sat in the chairs, rocking back and forth. One was huddled in a corner, knees drawn up to her chest, shaking her head, pointing up at the ceiling and then shaking more frantically. An attendant in a white pants suit sat at a brown metal desk, a phone to her ear, speaking Spanish with a grim expression.

His grandmother gestured to the attendant, spoke his mother's name. The woman shrugged and went back to her conversation. His grandmother asked the women against the wall where his mother was. When they gave her blank stares, his grandmother called his mother's name, loud, abrupt. Everyone stopped to look, then turned away.

An inner door swung open and his mother appeared. Gregory had to clutch at a chair back, suddenly chill, dizzy, the taste of his dinner rising into his throat. Her eyes were fixed, wide open and dark, her jaw clenched, teeth gritted, grinding back and forth, demanding, "Where are my cigarettes?" in the voice of Dr. Trapp.

His grandmother cowered, seemed to shrink as she dug into her purse to pull out one pack, two packs, then more, dropping them from her hands to the floor, stooping to retrieve them, and then holding them out to Gregory's mother like an offering.

Without thanks, his mother tore off a cellophane wrapper, crumpled it, and dug broken fingernails at a pack. In seconds other women surrounded her, reaching out, whining. A woman so fat she waddled shoved her way into the group, grabbing at the pack until others held down her thick arm. "Me, me," she shouted. His mother gave her a cigarette first, and the woman calmed; then she carefully passed cigarettes out to each of the others. The attendant laid the phone on the desk, frowned, and got up with a lighter. The women formed a line to suck at the flame. His mother waited, taking her turn last, glaring with a furious expression.

The other packs bulged from the pockets of the frayed sweater she wore. Gregory did not recognize it, nor her dress, short sleeved with faded flowers, much too large for her, hanging limp on her gaunt body.

His mother stepped in front of his grandmother, inhaled deeply, and blew smoke in her face. "Thank you very much for the smokes," she said, in a voice he had never heard before, clipped, chirping, like someone from England, but not real.

"Gregory!" she said suddenly, as if she had just realized he was there, in that room. She called out to the others with the same odd accent, "Everyone, this is my son. Come meet my son." She rubbed at his hair, hard, yanking. But he was afraid to flinch.

Fingers digging into his shoulder, she led him to the row of patients at the wall, stopping in front of an ancient woman with a back so crooked she stood doubled over. "This is Annie," his mother said. The woman stared out with fogged eyes that seemed to float in a pink fluid. Gregory thought she was blind. Then his mother leaned against his ear and spoke in the high wheedling voice he knew as Betty Jean. "Annie steals. She steals from all of us. Can't help it, poor thing."

His mother bumped him with her hip, forcing him toward the next person at the wall, a small coffee-colored woman with fuzz-like hair constantly moving, bobbing up and down with flexed knees, her head swiveling back and forth. She grinned with the gaping holes of missing teeth, but Gregory knew it was not for him.

He turned to his grandmother with a pleading look — take me away. But she had her hands to her face, shielding her eyes, as if she did not want to see.

His mother made him stop in front of the shaking woman, pointing down at her, said, "She can't talk," and forced out laughter, a hollow sound. Stop, he wanted to beg her. Stop!

The inner door drew back and a young woman stepped into the room. Her dress was neat, her hair combed, her nails a polished red. When she opened arms and reached out to his mother, Gregory thought she must be a doctor, the way she embraced his mother, making soft caring sounds.

"Jocelyn," his mother said, her voice almost normal, "this is my son. This is Gregory."

Smiling, Jocelyn pressed both his hands between her palms. "Gregory. What a wonderful name. I'm so pleased to know you."

"Thank you," he said, not sure what was happening. He heard his mother's voice, loud, as if making an announcement. "Jocelyn is my friend."

She cupped Gregory's face in her hands, looked deep into his eyes. "I'm so pleased to know a mother and her son."

The attendant was back on her feet, moving quickly from behind the desk, forcing herself between Jocelyn and Gregory. An arm around Jocelyn's waist, she led her toward the inner door. "Time to go back now."

Jocelyn paused in the doorway, tears in her eyes. "Gregory. I'd have known anywhere whose son you were. You are the image of her. Just like your mother."

As the door closed, his mother pressed at his side, leaning close, her lips at his ear, speaking as Dr. Trapp, the words harsh. "He's just like his mother!" She squeezed him tight, standing rigid, hurting him, his face forced into the sour wool of her sweater.

Gregory wrestled away, slapping at her hands, kicking her legs.

He rushed toward the corridor, past the shaking woman who beat fists against the wall. His grandmother shouted his name. Outside, slamming the door, he ran as fast as he could, then slipped on something wet, tumbling down and picking himself up to run again. But he felt himself being hoisted into the air, great hands locked under his arms. Gregory began writhing, and the hands held him away. "Easy now." He looked out to see the face of a large black man dressed in white, a name tag pinned to his coat.

He wouldn't let himself cry. "I don't want to be here."

"Nobody does," the man said.

His grandmother appeared, breathless, a hand on her chest. "You OK now?" the man asked, and when Gregory nodded, put him down on the floor tiles. Tightlipped, his grandmother seized his wrist. He expected her to thank the man. Always be polite, she had told him all his life. Now she said nothing, just hurried him away.

She turned into a long, empty corridor. He didn't remember having come this way. No people, no stink of cigarettes, just a narrow space with pale green walls and dim ceiling lights thick with dust.

He had to half run to keep up with her. Halfway down the corridor he saw a metal door with rows of shining rivets and wide hinges. A sign in red letters said "Keep Locked at All Times." He knew what that meant. This was where they put the people crazier than his mother. He could not imagine what was inside. The thought of it made him tremble, his body shaking so much he could not move a step.

Then he heard a sound like a screech, so awful it didn't seem human. Help! Help! He was only thinking the word. Who would hear? Who would help?

His grandmother tugged at his arm. "Come on. I'm taking you home."

In the car, headlights slicing into the darkness, she stayed silent. Small circles flashed along the roadside. Animal eyes. He wanted to ask her what Jocelyn had done, why she was there, but knew his grandmother would not tell him. He kept seeing the woman's face, hearing her words. The image of his mother. Just like her.

When they reached his house, his grandmother did not turn off the engine. "Go," she ordered. "Go inside." She drove off the second he closed the car door.

His father sat in darkness on the stiff wooden chair, a shadow in the moonlight. It seemed a great effort for him to speak. "Did you see your mother?"

"I'm not like her!" Gregory cried. "Not!"

Without turning on a light, he climbed the stairs to the second floor. In his bedroom, he groped hands along the wall until he found the closet. He slid inside, pulled the door closed behind him, slowly, until the lock clicked. Releasing the handle, he curled on the floorboards and groped behind shoe boxes until he found the string, squeezing it in his fist, winding it around his fingers, pulling tighter and tighter until he felt pain. Though the blackness was total, he stared out at nothing.

Little Old Man

When Warren made the decision to die, he worried most about his wife, Julia — what would happen to her alone in a house a car ride from the nearest stores. She hadn't driven in years, would never drive again, her spine warped like an S, constant knives of pain stabbing her back and legs and face, her mind addled from frequent doses of Percocet. He wouldn't be around to monitor her pills, couldn't do it now anyway, barely inching along with his walker, wincing at the hurt in his own legs when he took a step. How could he stop her from opening the medication drawer any time during the day and sleepless nights? Sometimes she would call to him with her slurred voice, "Warren, did I take my pills?" He pictured her tongue wobbling in her mouth like a guppy on a table. "Yes," he would shout, "just an hour ago." But he would hear the drawer slide, the water run.

What would happen to her? He, ten years older, had been taking care of her for decades of her sufferings: first the swollen legs, then the rheumatoid arthritis, the scoliosis, the agony of tic douloureux. Teeth pulled, alcohol injected into nerves, procedure after procedure, specialist after specialist, to deaden the pain. Nothing worked. And now he was the one gravely ill, everything falling apart within months: a trickle of circulation below the knees, congestive heart failure, barely any kidney function. The EMTs call me every night before I call them, he told people. It seemed like every few weeks they had to rush him to Emergency for a lung pumping. "What else can I expect?" he would say, surprised that it was finally happening. "Hell, I'm an old man."

•

A little old man. A small boy had called him that even when he was still mobile, driving himself around the neighborhood. He had gone to take a book to his friend Stan, a man he had known for fifty years. The boy answered the door chimes, no more than six or seven. When Warren asked for Stan, the boy called back, "Hey, Grandpa, there's a little old man here to see you." Warren laughed out loud right on the spot, gripping Stan's arm when he appeared and still laughing. "Did you hear that? Damn it! The kid's right." Back home, Warren stood in front of a mirror and really looked at himself. There he was, grey and shrunken, his flesh ashen, loose on his face, his muscles just flab. "Goddamn!" he said aloud, amazed at what he had become. That night he called and ordered the boy a toy race car, asked that the card be signed "From the Little Old Man."

"Look at me," he said to Julia. "What do you see?" "You," she told him, "just you." She didn't recognize how he had changed, didn't care. He realized he was relieved that she was spared knowing. Dying was his problem, not hers. She lived for her pain killers, constantly checking the family room clock, sitting in her orthopedic chair just feet from the TV, the sound loud, but barely paying attention. She would talk over the sound, mentioning his name now and then, but really a monologue about things that had happened with her mother and father and sister a lifetime ago, agitated as she relived the same handful of days over and over.

●

Of course, Warren didn't blame the boy, but soon after he was identified as a little old man, he began becoming one, not deliberately, actually trying to will himself backwards, forcing himself to get out of the house, visit friends, attend meetings of his clubs. But the more he did, the more exhausted he felt, drifting off in his easy chair soon after supper, waking with a start at midnight, momentarily unsure where he was, then seeing Julia squinting at the TV screen, wondering how he could have slept with the speakers blaring.

His legs had been the first sign of disintegration, the poor circulation. For quite a while, they had been cramping when he walked the length of a block, and he had to stop to rest, knead the calves. Now he could barely get from the house to the car without a painful hobbling. His heart function declined from fifty percent of normal to thirty, and he had to take strong medications. But his kidneys were the most severe problem. For a decade, they had been weakening, and his doctor warned him that if his creatinine count went any higher, he would need dialysis.

•

The procedure piqued his curiosity. Warren read pamphlets and tried to imagine the process. Fortunately, a dialysis center was available just five minutes from his house, and he could still drive. The treatment took three hours. One of a dozen patients, he sat tilted back in a molded chair hooked to a machine that droned a dull whirring. On a TV suspended from a wall bracket, contestants screamed at one another, the audience cheering and hooting. Warren spread a magazine on his lap but rarely read, eventually getting into conversations with the other patients lined up on two sides of the room, realizing he was by far the oldest of the group. Some, in fact, were very young, and he felt sorry for the years they faced. They talked about families and children, he relieved that his son was a continent away, his life and work there, too busy to be tied down by his parents' poor health. It wouldn't be fair, he realized, while he bragged about Richard's career, his promotions. Old people should fend for themselves, he declared. They've enjoyed their best years and had no right to rob others of theirs.

But the dialysis became more excruciating with each treatment, the machine drawing the fluid out of him so severely his sinews cramped into knots of agony. He clenched teeth, breathless, in spasm. The technician sympathized: "That's the way it happens at your stage." "Then," Warren told him, "it's no stage to be at." The technician just looked away.

Three times a week, home after dialysis, he could barely move from all the aches in his body, sitting in a chair and panting, unable to lift the newspaper or focus on the screen ten feet away. The next day he would sleep till noon, eat a slice of bread, and doze on and off till the evening, then lie awake, dreading the thought of enduring another treatment.

"This is no life," he finally admitted to Julia after several months of misery, wanting to spare her but finally having to say it aloud.

"At least you're alive," she told him.

"What if I wasn't?"

"What would happen to me?"

"I don't know." He touched her hand, the swollen knuckles, the brittle skin.

The conversation ended, but he continued it in his mind. What was he doing for her now? Driving slowly to a store for food and prescriptions, opening cans for meals she rarely ate and he had to force himself to swallow. One day, very soon, he wouldn't even be able to do that.

•

The accident convinced him. He was backing out of his driveway, a maneuver he had been making for years, when he lost control and shot across the street, smashing his taillight and knocking over a neighbor's mailbox. He apologized, wrote a check, and made it to his treatment. But when he drove home, he was trembling, afraid to creep faster than five miles an hour, a black SUV behind him blasting its horn. A month before he would have cursed the driver. Now tears steamed down his face. "I can't do this any more," he kept saying, "can't." Right there, behind the wheel, a block from home on the most familiar street he had ever known, he decided to die.

•

Warren called his doctor to be sure what would happen if he stopped dialysis. "You'll get uremia and poison yourself," the doctor told him. "How long could I live that way?" Warren asked. "Three or four days. Why?" "Just curious," Warren said.

The first day he missed his dialysis appointment, he held himself tense in his chair, as if he would never get up again. Julia was prowling the house, hunched and twisted, dragging one foot as she moved from room to room, opening cabinets, slamming drawers. "Where's my pills?" he could hear her say each time she entered a room, going in and out the same doors several times, searching the same cabinets. The third time she returned to the family room, she gave Warren a look of surprise. "Are you supposed to be here?"

"I live here."

"Shouldn't you be somewhere?"

"Not any more."

"Whatever you say. Where's my pills?"

"Wherever you left them."

"If I knew that, I wouldn't be asking you." She moved into the kitchen.

Although he felt too weak too laugh, hurt too much, Warren knew that a stranger watching them might think it was comical—two old people having a ridiculous conversation, barely functioning, no thoughts beyond their hurts and their ailments. When he tried to look out into the family room, his vision was blurred, everything behind a grey film. But he knew what was there on the paneled walls, framed pictures of him and Julia when they were younger, faces touching, smiles broad, their son as a boy. Memories of a lifetime that he didn't care about recalling now. He wasn't even a little old man any more. Little old corpse, he kept thinking, the words swirling in his brain, a dimness spinning before his eyes, until he saw nothing.

•

When Warren looked out again, the light was dazzling, pouring in through the open Venetian blinds of a strange room, bright metal objects all around him, a pouch of liquid dangling from a steel stand, a tube in his arm. Hospital, he knew. And when he turned his head, there was Richard leaning over him with a rigid smile. "Hi, Dad."

"How'd you get here?"

"Airplane. The way I always do."

Warren made an effort to return the smile, not sure if his face were still functioning. Richard seemed so big, so strong and youthful, though he was a man close to sixty. It pleased Warren to see him and, once again, he realized how proud he was of his son, how much he had awaited his weekly phone calls, the sound of his voice. Richard was holding his hand, gripping it in a gesture of shaking, but pressing down with the other, the warmth of contact.

"You shouldn't have had to come," he said. "I didn't want you to see this."

"If not your son, then who?"

"Nobody. Nobody should see this. People should wander off into the woods like animals."

"People have other people who care about them."

"That's sad. In the long run, love is sad."

Richard was shaking his head, pressing his hand harder. "Only for a fraction of time. The rest it's good."

"How did you know I was here?"

"Mom called. It took me a while to figure out what she was saying. She must have swallowed a fistful of Percocet. But I finally understood that you weren't moving, barely breathing. So I called the EMTs and booked the next flight."

"What's going to happen to her?" Warren asked.

"What's going to happen to you?" Richard said, his tone flat, as if stating a technical dilemma. Warren smiled, once again surprised that he had produced an engineer.

"Not what," he said. "When. No more dialysis. I know you won't try to get me to change my mind."

"I wish I could."

"What good would that do?"

"None." Richard pinched the corners of his eyes and looked away.

Warren felt his head sink into the pillow, too heavy to lift, his throat dry as sand. He gestured to Richard for ice water, a wet towel pressed to his lips as he sucked on the cloth. "The funeral's all paid for. Five years ago. You'll find the papers in the top drawer of my desk. All the arrangements. My lawyer has the will. A couple of phone calls. That's the only thing you'll have to do. It's your mother we have to talk about."

"I'm not taking her with us. Don't make me promise that, Dad. All she talks about is her pain. I guess she has a right to do that as much as she hurts. But I have a right not to be around it any more too. So does Bonnie."

Wait till you're a little old man and she's a little old lady, Warren thought, but didn't say it, knowing it wouldn't be fair. Let him find out when it happens. His eyelids felt so heavy. As much as he tried to force them apart, he drifted into greyness.

•

Each time he lost consciousness, Warren expected never to wake again. *This is it.* He heard those words in his head, elongated, like a record on an old windup phonograph with a rundown spring. That was the image that occurred to him when he woke up again, seeing a memory of the first one he had every owned, hearing snatches of tunes. But it was all scattered, one picture fading into the next, people and places from decades apart flowing in and out of his consciousness. He couldn't make them hold still, couldn't will himself to focus on any one.

This wasn't what he expected, not what he had read about dying. No bright light luring him to another realm, no sensation of crossing a threshold. There was no other realm. For him, nothing but this room— the steel bars of the bed, the bulbs in the ceiling, the weight of the blanket that covered him. If he tried, he could think of Julia wandering through the house, opening cabinets, rummaging through drawers. But it all seemed so far away, a tiny image at the end of a tunnel.

When the nurses came into the room, checking his catheter, renewing the pain killer, sponging his body, rolling him this way and that to change sheets, he was alert, flirting with the young ones, teasing the old. He would gesture toward the morphine drip with a lifting of his chin. "Great stuff. I should have known about this years ago." His voice was thin. Some of the nurses smiled. One patted his hand. "Years ago they would have locked you up." "If you came by every day," he said, "it would have been worth it."

When his doctor looked in, Warren asked what day it was. "Thursday," the doctor told him. "I mean day without dialysis." The doctor looked at his watch. "Fifth."

"I thought I was supposed to be dead by now."

"How bad is the pain?"

Warren winced and swallowed. "What pain?"

"There's still time to change your mind."

"A lot of good that would do."

"You're a tough old bird."

"Just a little old man."

•

Richard seemed to be in the room more and more. At least, whenever Warren awoke and looked up, his son was there, standing over him or sitting on a chair beside the bed.

"You don't have to come here so much," Warren told him.

"I want to be with you."

"Dying is boring. It must be more boring to watch."

"I'll miss you, Dad."

"Since you were born, it's been a treat just to think about you, to know you exist." Warren turned toward the window. "Is the sun out?"

"Dazzling. Do you want me to close the blinds?"

"Everything I look at now is in a haze."

Richard lifted Warren's hand, studied it. "Your fingertips are purple now, cold."

"I'm behind schedule. So much for medical predictions." Warren tried to look at his own fingers but saw only a blur. "What does your mother say?"

"She keeps asking when you're coming home. She's angry that you're away."

"What about her pills?"

"I locked them up. Give them to her on the prescribed schedule."

"That's what she's really mad about. Any ideas about what's to become of her?"

"I checked out a nursing home." Richard described the facility — the size of a private room where she could have her own furniture, the dining room, the nursing care, the monthly costs, but Warren couldn't hold on to the details. It sounded fine.

"She won't go," he said. "You'd have to tie her up and drag her out of the house." He imagined Julia shrieking, her warped body thrashing, summing up great strength in a furious resistance. Desperate to survive, obsessed with her Percocet. A strange life force.

•

Warren felt himself trembling, then realized there was a hand on his shoulder, light, barely pressing down. "Dad, Dad," he heard and turned his head to look up at Richard's face bending over him, just inches away.

Hi, he wanted to say, but it came out as a groan, a sound so quiet he wasn't sure his son heard.

"Dad. Mom's here."

"What?" Warren tried to lift his head and see the room. "Where?" He didn't want to see her, not in this place.

"In a room down the hall."

In an instant his mind cleared, as if a great rock had been lifted from his brain. "Why? What happened?" Now he could hear his own voice.

"She overdosed. She must have hidden some pills. I was getting into bed when I heard a loud crash from her room. When I found her on the floor, I thought she was dead. The rescue squad came in no time. They pumped her out in Emergency and brought her up here. That was last night."

"What is it now?"

"Past noon. You've been sleeping for hours."

"Did she do it on purpose?"

"I don't think so. I've been rationing her. She's been greedy for those damn pills. Probably found her stash and gulped them down. The hospital won't keep her overnight now. Insurance. I have to get her out by evening."

Warren strained to think, to made sense of it all. Both of them in the same hospital, on the same floor. It was crazy. Maybe it wasn't happening, just a delusion from all the poison in his body. The kidneys weren't filtering. Gone loony from his own waste and a morphine drip. He spoke his son's name — "Richard" — to see if he was truly there. When Richard answered, he knew what to say. "Take your mother straight to that nursing home. Hire an ambulance. Have them lash her to a stretcher so she can't get away. Somebody has to take care of her."

"I already made arrangements."

Warren tried to smile. "We think alike."

"She wants to see you," Richard said. "Cursing the nurses because they won't bring her down the hall. That's one reason they're so eager to get rid of her."

About to protest, to say, no, not like this, Warren realized it didn't matter any more. He shrugged. "Why not?"

•

He must have slept again, because when Warren opened his eyes at a shrill squeaking sound, it was dark outside the window, a ceiling light reflecting in the glass. He heard his name, Julia's voice, then Richard's. A nurse had wheeled her gurney right beside his bed, his wife stretched out alongside him, wrapped in a white sheet, fixed to the flat surface with dark straps.

When he looked out to her, he didn't see her, not as she was now, but his memory from decades before, shining brown hair, brilliant dark eyes, the joy in her face as she smiled at their child. He reached out an arm, barely able to extend it in his weakness. A hand touched his. It might have been hers. "Isn't she the prettiest thing?" he said to the nurse.

He heard them rolling her away and Julia calling back, insisting, "You'd better come visit me," and his son squeezing his hand, touching his face as he stepped away.

Even before they were out the door, Warren closed his eyes and knew it was over.

Walter Cummins has published five other short story collections—*Witness, Where We Live, Local Music, The End of the Circle, The Lost Ones.* and *Habitat: stories of bent realism.* More than 100 of his stories, as well as memoirs, essays, and reviews, have appeared in magazines such as *Kansas Quarterly, Virginia Quarterly Review, Under the Sun, Confrontation, Bellevue Literary Review, Connecticut Review, The Laurel Review, Other Voices, Georgetown Review, Contrary, Sonora Review, Abiko Quarterly, Weber Studies, Midwest Quarterly, West Branch, South Carolina Review, Crosscurrents, Crescent Review, The MacGuffin,* in book collections, and on the Web. With Thomas E. Kennedy, he is co-publisher of Serving House Books, an outlet for novels, story collections, poetry, and essays. For more than twenty years, he was editor of *The Literary Review.* He teaches in Fairleigh Dickinson University's MFA in Creative Writing Program.